"I didn't expect to find you waiting."

Luke's voice was sardonic. Sally was hurt by the cynicism in his eyes.

"I was worried," she said unsteadily.

"Ah, I see," he mocked. "You imagined an accident, eh? No doubt you've been waiting breathlessly for confirmation of my injuries—or worse." His laugh was without humor. "Tell me, my darling, would you have shed tears over my death?"

Sally shivered as he firmly turned her to face him. "Don't call me that!" she flung at him. "I'm not your darling. I never was and I never will be!"

He pulled her close against him. "You are the other half of me, *carina*, do you not know that?" He smiled down teasingly. "Though there were times when I'd have liked to wring your neck!"

Other titles by

HELEN BIANCHIN
IN HARLEQUIN PRESENTS

Other titles by

HELEN BIANCHIN
IN HARLEQUIN PRESENTS

◆

Many of these titles, and other titles in the Harlequin
Romance series, are available at your local
bookseller or through the Harlequin Reader Service.
For a free catalogue listing all available Harlequin
Presents and Harlequin Romances, send your name
and address to:

HARLEQUIN READER SERVICE
M.P.O. Box 707,
Niagara Falls, N.Y. 14302
Canadian address:
Stratford, Ontario, Canada N5A 6W2
or use coupon at back of book.

HELEN BIANCHIN

stormy possession

Harlequin Books

TORONTO • LONDON • NEW YORK • AMSTERDAM
SYDNEY • HAMBURG • PARIS

Harlequin Presents edition published June 1979
ISBN 0-373-70789-4

Original hardcover edition published in 1979
by Mills & Boon Limited

Copyright © 1979 by Helen Bianchin. All rights reserved.
Philippine copyright 1979. Australian copyright 1979.
Except for use in any review, the reproduction or utilization of
this work in whole or in part in any form by any electronic,
mechanical or other means, now known or hereafter invented,
including xerography, photocopying and recording, or in any
information storage or retrieval system, is forbidden
without the permission of the publisher.

All the characters in this book have no existence outside the
imagination of the author and have no relation whatsoever to
anyone bearing the same name or names. They are not even
distantly inspired by any individual known or unknown to the
author, and all the incidents are pure invention.

The Harlequin trademark, consisting of the word HARLEQUIN
and the portrayal of a Harlequin, is registered in the United States
Patent Office and in the Canada Trade Marks Office.

Printed in U.S.A

CHAPTER ONE

SALLY raised her head with a feeling of regret as the radio D.J.'s voice announced the time. Stretching out a hand she switched off the transistor, then gracefully moved to sit hugging her knees as she gazed out over the ocean.

Chinaman's Beach at the end of Shell Cove was a delightful spot—particularly during the week. Weekends, when most everyone flocked to the many bays and coves abounding Sydney's wandering harbour waters, were a different matter entirely.

It had to be the hottest summer on record, she mused idly. These past few hours spent lazily sunbathing had been positively idyllic, for with Christmas mere weeks away, the city was choked with traffic and the pavements crammed with jostling shoppers.

With one fluid movement she stood to her feet, slipped off her sunglasses and tossed them down on to the beach towel. She felt unbearably hot, and the sea's coolness was infinitely inviting. With light steps she ran to the water, delighting in its silkiness against her body, and she lingered in the shallows for several minutes before emerging again.

The two minuscule scraps of material covering her slim curves were inclined to reveal more than they concealed, although she had no pretensions about her appearance and didn't consider her combination of shoulder-length silver-blonde hair, a slim shapely figure, golden-brown skin, and eyes of deep blue to be anything startling, despite her father's teasing remarks on occasion to the contrary.

Dear Daddy, Sally reflected fondly. It didn't seem anything like eight years since she'd left school and moved in to share his apartment in suburban Rose Bay. An only child, her parents had separated while she was still in kindergarten, and after the divorce she had been consigned to boarding school. Vacations were alternately spent at her mother's chic Double Bay flat and the Rose Bay apartment. Luckily, she had never been the bone over which her parents fought for possession, and to all intents and purposes her parents had maintained an amicable relationship. But just when she most needed a woman's hand, her mother impulsively remarried and moved to America, leaving Sally to cope as best she could with the vulnerable teenage years. After completion of her formal education there followed a two-year catering course from which she emerged with honours, and in the past six years she'd graduated from lowly kitchen maid to assistant chef with one of Sydney's exclusive catering firms.

Sally shook off her reverie as she reached the sand where her belongings lay, and she picked up her brush to restore a measure of order to her salt-tangled hair. Its length was a nuisance in summer, but she liked its versatility, and inevitably wound it on top of her head whenever she hovered twixt stove and work-bench.

A hasty glance at her wristwatch as she strapped it on declared a need to abandon any thoughts of sunbathing to dry out her bikini. Not that it really mattered, for it would dry as she drove home. In a few minutes she had dismantled the beach-umbrella in readiness, and picking up her transistor, towel, and paperback, she thrust them into her bag. With sunglasses slid on to her nose, her feet thrust into leather sandals, she was ready to leave.

The racy MGB-GT sports saloon that had been a twenty-first birthday gift from her father stood parked on the grass verge some distance away, and Sally headed towards it, her thoughts becoming pensive as she went over the menu she'd planned for tonight. Onion soup then *coq-au-vin*, with strawberry mousse for dessert. Most of the preparation had been done that morning, but she needed an hour of unflustered concentration to do the food justice.

Joseph Ballinger—Joe, to his friends—was an extremely active man, socially. A builder by trade, he ran his own business, and delighted in entertaining, giving as many as two dinner parties a month—sometimes more.

This evening's event was only one of many that Sally had catered for, and her brow furrowed as she endeavoured to recollect the guests' names. Oscar and Olivia Nordestein, a charming middle-aged couple who were frequent guests at her father's table. Charles and Andrea Bakersfield, and their daughter Chantrelle.

On reaching the car, Sally stowed everything on to the back seat, then slid in behind the wheel and headed towards the city. The breeze set up by the car's movement was refreshing on her warm skin, teasing strands of damp hair and lifting them away from her neck. Heavens, it was hot! Leaning forward, she slid open the ventilator in an effort to increase the air-flow into the car's interior.

The road wound round numerous bays as it followed the coast, and all too soon she was in the midst of traffic crossing the metal girth of Sydney's harbour bridge. Never once did the sight of the Opera House fail to cause her to catch her breath, with its concrete sails peaking in a unique feat of architecture, set close to the deep sparkling waters of Port Jackson.

Sally eased the car on to New South Head Road, and was almost adjacent to the golf links at Rose Bay when she became aware of the erratic behaviour of her MGB-GT. Not a puncture, she pleaded silently—without heed, it proved, for there was no mistaking that lopsided thudding. With a sigh of resignation she flicked the indicator and pulled into the kerb, then slid out from behind the wheel to inspect the car's rear.

A few muttered epithets whispered from her lips as she unlocked the boot and began shifting tools and nameless junk in an effort to uncover the spare tyre.

'Can I be of assistance?'

Sally turned slowly to face the owner of that deep drawl, and her eyes widened fractionally as they took in the rugged, sardonic features of the man standing a few feet distant. Hairs tingled down the length of her spine as she registered shock at the sheer animal magnetism he projected. Even his conservative business suit did little to sheathe a raw masculinity that sent shivers of apprehension scudding in countless different directions. There was a dangerous compelling quality about him that made her want to run and hide.

'I have changed a tyre on at least two previous occasions,' she managed coolly, and turned away in the hope that he would take the hint and leave her to her own resources.

'I didn't stop merely to *watch* your feminine efforts,' he retorted with soft emphasis, and there was a faint accent, more an intonation of certain vowels, that was attractive to the ear.

'By all means, go ahead,' she declared sarcastically, and moved to one side, conscious for the first time of her brief attire.

One dark eyebrow lifted in cynical amusement as he

shrugged off an immaculately-tailored jacket, and Sally suppressed a start of surprise when he held it out towards her. 'If you don't mind?'

She took it from him, holding it in front of her like a protective shield—although why, she wasn't sure! The material felt expensive to the touch, and emitted an elusive male fragrance. Thoroughly cross with herself, she transferred her gaze to the car parked close behind her own, and noted the discreet Alfa-Romeo insignia on the grill of the sleek saloon.

In a remarkably short space of time he had the spare tyre in place, and Sally murmured a few polite words as he slung the punctured wheel into the boot.

He gave a negligent shrug and wiped his hands on a rag he extracted from among the debris. 'In your delectable state of déshabille, you had only to wait for as long as it took the first male to drive by,' he intimated dryly, and his eyes ran mockingly over her body, lingering with lazy insolence on her scantily-covered bosom. He took his jacket from her nerveless fingers, then leaning out a hand he ran a light finger over the exposed swell of her breast. 'I believe you have caught the sun.'

His fleeting touch scorched her skin, and she withdrew as sharply as if from a lick of flame. 'How dare you!' she whispered furiously. It was too late to wish she'd donned the muslin top she'd hastily flung on to the passenger seat of her car more than four hours before. Her only thought had been to remain cool in the intense heat during the drive home—modesty had been a secondary consideration, and unfortunately unheeded!

His soft laugh served to increase her outrage, and she had the distinct impression he would dare anything.

'*Ciao, bionda.*' With a sardonic wave he turned and walked to his car.

Sally slammed the boot shut and moved round to slip in behind the wheel. Her breathing was as ragged as if she'd just run a mile. Of all the infuriating, arrogant men she'd ever met, this one took the prize! His maddening words echoed inside her brain—she could translate the mockingly-voiced 'blondie' without too much effort! She pointedly didn't acknowledge the klaxon salute as he eased the Alfa-Romeo into the steady stream of traffic, and she deliberately waited several minutes before attempting to follow him.

Sally was still seething as she parked the car and walked up the two flights of stairs to her father's apartment. Selecting a key from the collection on her key-ring, she inserted it into the lock and stepped into the lobby.

'Hi—I'm home,' she called out as she shut the door behind her, and then as no one answered she moved through the lounge towards the kitchen. Ten minutes later the casserole containing the *coq-au-vin* was in the oven, and the ingredients for the soup were on the work-bench in readiness. Now for a quick shower, she decided silently.

In her room she thrust off the muslin top, then moved into the adjoining bathroom, emerging a short while later to slip into fresh underwear. She selected a printed jersey-silk patio dress from the wardrobe in her bedroom, stepped into it and slid the zip-fastener into place. Ten minutes with the blow-dryer and her hair was dry enough to wind into a knot on top of her head. A quick application of skin moisturiser, a touch of lipstick, eyeshadow and mascara to heighten her eyes, and her make-up was complete. There, that would do, she decided, casting her reflection a cursory glance in the mirror.

Philip would think she looked eye-catching, no matter what she wore. Sally hid a slight grimace. Quite what she was going to do about Philip eluded her, for he had become increasingly persistent in his attentions of late, and over the past few months he'd proposed marriage with predictable regularity. Why then did she hesitate to accept? She gave a sigh that defied description. Was it so wrong to want her emotions stirred into such a state of excitability that she couldn't even *think* straight? Was there a man, somewhere, meant for her alone, like the other half of a twin soul? Or were such things confined only between the pages of romantic novels, with no real-life parallel?

A knock at her bedroom door brought a return to the present, and calling out that she was ready, Sally emerged into the hall.

'Philip is here,' Joe Ballinger informed her, and she gave a monosyllabic acknowledgment. 'Ah, you look beautiful, my dear.'

Sally stood on tiptoe and kissed his chin. 'And you look very handsome, Daddy.' She tucked her hand through his arm, smiling up at him. 'Give Philip a drink. I'm needed in the kitchen for a while.'

Joe gave a slight chuckle. 'I rather think he'd prefer to be in the kitchen with you. The Nordesteins and the Bakersfields aren't due to arrive for at least another thirty minutes.'

They reached the lounge, and at once a tall, good-looking young man in his mid-twenties came forward with arms outstretched.

'There you are, darling.' He leant down and bestowed a fond kiss to her temple. 'Looking utterly gorgeous, as always.'

'Flattery will get you a glass of sherry,' Sally evinced gaily. 'Talk to Daddy, there's a few things I have to attend to in the kitchen.' She slipped away with an adroitness that brought a frown to Philip's forehead, and in the kitchen she took a deep breath. Dear God, what was wrong with her? Why tonight, of all nights, did she have to lapse into such a mood of introspection?

With deft fingers she prepared the soup and put it on the stove, checked the casserole, then slipped into the dining-room and began setting the table.

She soon became lost to the task in front of her, delighting in utilising her culinary skills to their fullest extent as she slid dishes from the oven and attended to saucepans simmering on top of the stove. Only when everything was placed into serving dishes to keep warm did she emerge into the lounge and accept the drink her father held out.

'Sally, how charming you look,' Andrea Bakersfield complimented her warmly. 'You must let me have your secret of appearing to remain so cool in the kitchen on so hot an evening.'

'Wear the minimum of clothes, and apply mind over matter,' Sally responded with a ready smile.

'Mother,' Chantrelle mocked gently as her eyes swept over Sally's slender form. 'You never go into the kitchen, so the question is entirely irrelevant.' She laughed with false gaiety as her eyes came to rest on Sally's head. 'Why, Sally dear, has preparing dinner been too much of a rush? Your hair is damp.'

'It's a secret of mine,' Sally responded with bitter-sweet politeness. 'That way I can remain cool.'

'What culinary delights have you planned to titillate our palates with tonight, my dear?'

Sally turned towards Olivia Nordestein with relief,

for Chantrelle, even in small doses, was too much to endure. 'I've made strawberry mousse for dessert,' she said lightly. 'As to what preludes it, that will have to remain a surprise.'

'You look strangely unsettled tonight,' Philip murmured as he crossed to her side, and she forced a bright smile to her lips.

'I've been at the beach for a few hours. Perhaps the sun?' she suggested.

'I have tickets for the opera tomorrow evening. Will you come?'

She looked into his earnest, transparent face, and didn't have the heart to refuse. 'Thank you, I'd like that.'

His features broadened into a relaxed, relieved smile. 'I'll call for you at seven. We'll have dinner first.'

Tomorrow she'd probably view things differently, but now it took an effort to be considerate of his feelings, and she hated the little gremlin that was sitting on her shoulder. With a slight smile she excused herself and went into the kitchen to serve the soup while Joe bade his guests seat themselves in the dining-room.

The soup was a delight, and the *coq-au-vin* faultless. Sally gave her father a quick smile as he complimented her skill.

'Dear Sally, talented in so many things,' Chantrelle extolled sweetly. 'I can't even boil water—but then I shall never have to, shall I?' She made a pouting moue, and let her eyes sweep slowly round the table.

'If you're of the social élite, there's always the restaurant on cook's night off,' Sally commented, and the other girl gave a trill of light laughter.

'Of course, sweetie. I don't plan on doing anything more strenuous than being a glamorous partner to a wealthy husband.'

'A millionaire, without doubt, to cater to your expensive tastes?'

'At the very least,' Chantrelle asserted with glittering emphasis. 'There are still some around.'

'I shall pray the one you snare isn't balding, paunchy, and over fifty,' Sally ventured with false sweetness, and Chantrelle pouted prettily.

'One can suffer a lot with silken sheets on the bed, mink on one's back, and jewels for every occasion.'

'I think I'll serve dessert,' Sally declared with a tight smile. In another minute she'd say something really catty!

'My compliments—that was superb.'

Sally inclined her head slightly in Philip's direction, but didn't meet his eyes. The mousse had turned out well, she knew, but she was darned if she would simper appreciatively beneath his praise.

'As usual, an exquisite meal, my dear,' Joe added fondly, then he waved an expansive hand to encompass his guests. 'If you would all like to adjourn to the lounge?'

'While dear little Cinderella attends to the dishes,' Chantrelle ventured sweetly, blandly ignoring the angry gasps from her parents.

'It's not as bad as that,' Sally laughed—what else could she do but laugh? If she resorted to a baser feminine instinct she'd grab a handful of Chantrelle's hair and pull—hard! 'I have a magic genie in the form of an automatic dishwasher—in no time at all the kitchen will be restored to order.'

Nevertheless, Chantrelle's barbs struck home, and Sally scoured the innumerable saucepans with unnecessary diligence considering they were to go into the diswasher, but the exercise served to expend some of her anger.

It was well after eleven when the Bakersfields and the Nordesteins took their leave, and Sally turned to Philip with an apologetic smile.

'Goodnight,' she bade gently, trying hard to ignore the look of disappointment in his eyes. 'I have a headache from being out in the sun, and besides, it's rather late.' She held up her face for his kiss, and felt the warm, faintly moist mouth descend on hers. Oh, why can't I feel something when he kisses me? she tormented herself guiltily. He could have been a brother, or a fond cousin, for all the feeling his touch aroused.

When the door was firmly shut, Sally gave a heartfelt sigh of relief.

'Tired, my dear?'

Sally looked fondly at her father and smiled. 'A little. I'm afraid Chantrelle rubs me the wrong way—I find it difficult to retain a sense of cool whenever she's around.'

He quirked a quizzical eyebrow. 'And Philip? Have you two disagreed about something? You seemed to be consciously avoiding him tonight.'

'Was it obvious?' she queried ruefully. 'It must be the heat, and Christmas being so close—perhaps I need a holiday.'

'End-of-the-year blues? I feel a little jaded myself.'

'You worry too much,' Sally scolded, looking at her father closely. There were lines around his eyes, and tiny furrows creasing his forehead that she hadn't noticed before. Come to think of it, he didn't look terribly well. His colour wasn't good, despite the tanned leathery look acquired from working out of doors exposed to the elements. There was a greyish tinge around his mouth that disturbed her.

Before her eyes, he began to crumple, sinking slowly until with an anguished cry she caught hold of him and managed to get him into a chair.

'My pills—drawer beside bed,' Joe gasped breathlessly, and she ran, her fingers fumbling in her haste to unscrew the bottle.

One, the labelled prescription instructed, and she pressed it between his lips, then raced into the kitchen for some water for him to swallow it down.

The effect was miraculous, and when he had regained most of his colour, she fixed him with a firm stare. 'Now, suppose you tell me what this is all about?'

He gave her a weak smile. 'It looks much worse than it actually is.'

'How long have you been taking these?' she persisted quietly, holding the bottle of pills aloft. At his answering silence, she said gently, 'I love you. Haven't I a right to know?'

Joe gave a resigned nod that did little to relieve her anxiety. 'Yes, I owe you that much. Months, Sally. No,' he held up a hand as she gave a cry of distress, 'I've several years ahead of me yet. I keep bottles of these pills everywhere,' he smiled in an attempt at humour. 'Home, work, in the car—I even carry them around with me.'

'Wouldn't it be better if you retired from work?' she suggested anxiously, and glimpsed his wry grimace. A tiny seed of doubt began worrying its way through her brain. It was a well-known fact that many small businesses were closing down owing to an insufficient liquidity flow caused by the widespread economic situation. Her father had a few assets, she knew, but if he had borrowed heavily against these, he could be in trouble. Added to which he liked to gamble —cards, and the racetrack. He need only to have had a succession of losses to be in financial straits. Worriedly, she ventured, 'Are things very bad?'

Joe Ballinger's eyes assumed a bleak expression and his whole frame seemed to sag. He looked at her, then said quietly, 'In a way I'm glad you've guessed. It was doubtful I could have kept it from you much longer.'

Sally felt a strange sense of foreboding. 'Are you in some kind of trouble?' she queried gently, and he nodded.

'I need money, Sally. Rather a lot of money, I'm afraid.'

'There's my savings,' she offered swiftly. 'And my car.'

'Thank you, my dear,' he acknowledged gently, shaking his head. 'Only it wouldn't make any appreciable difference.'

'You own this apartment—there's the business. Surely one of the banks would give you a loan?'

'I'm already over-committed to them,' he revealed wearily. 'The building business is so slow that new contracts are almost negligible. I've taken a few uncalculated risks which have rebounded with a vengeance.'

'There are other lending institutions——' she began, but his silent headshake brought her to a halt.

'I've tried them all.'

She endeavoured to be sensible. 'What happens now?'

He gave a heartfelt sigh. 'The bank will foreclose, my creditors will sue, and Andretti will see me bankrupt.'

Oh dear God, it was worse than she thought. Much worse. 'Andretti?' she queried aloud. 'Who is he?'

'A high-powered business consultant and financier —extremely successful, and,' he paused fractionally— 'a more uncompromising man I have yet to meet.'

Sally's eyes clouded and became serious. 'I take it he's issued some sort of ultimatum?'

'You could say that,' Joe evinced wryly. 'I have an appointment with my solicitor tomorrow, after which it's a certainty wheels will be put into motion towards my becoming an adjudged bankrupt.' He gave a fatalistic sigh, and spread his hands in a gesture of utter weariness. 'Everything will have to go.'

A germ of an idea formed in her mind. It was possible—just barely possible, admittedly, but—'Can you postpone seeing your solicitor until Wednesday?' she pleaded, adding, 'An extra day won't make any difference, will it?'

The look he cast her was infinitely curious. 'What do you have in mind, Sally? I assure you I've tried every source available.'

'I'm not even sure it will work,' she had to admit. 'But it's worth a try.'

He shrugged wearily, and Sally was struck by the fatigue and desperation evident in his face. He looked a tired, broken man, older than his years.

'Now,' she hastened briskly, smiling at him, 'you must go to bed. I'll lock up and attend to the lights.' Already her mind was occupied with what she must do the following day. Philip might be able to help, but failing that she would confront Mr Andretti. Thank heavens she didn't have to report to work until midday tomorrow.

Sally slept badly, and woke cursing the strident summons of her alarm clock, set for seven to give her an early start to the day.

Her father appeared to have shared the same fate, for his eyes were faintly bloodshot and showed definite signs of a sleepless night. Despite any remon-

strances she made, he left shortly before eight o'clock
declaring a need to check some matters with his fore-
man.

Almost as soon as the apartment door closed behind
him, Sally flew to the telephone and dialled Philip's
number with impatient fingers.

His delight turned to incredulity as she explained
her father's predicament, and any hope she might have
cherished died an instant death. Dear cautious Philip
—how little she really knew him! He had, he assured
her, nothing like the amount she requested. His assests
were all carefully invested to provide a comfortable in-
come, and his share of the substantial capital involved
in his father's business formed part of a trust he could
not touch. His reasons for not helping seemed carefully contrived, and she could almost sense his panic
emanating down the wire. After several seconds she
said with a calmness she was far from feeling,

'I take it you aren't able to help?'

'Sally——' his voice was an ill-concealed splutter,
and she experienced a feeling of helplessness. 'it's not
that I don't want to—I simply can't put my hands on
so large an amount of money. My father——'

'Would never sanction it,' she interrupted hollowly.
'It's all right, Philip, I understand.'

He assumed a conciliatory tone. 'A lot of small
firms are going under, Sally. There's not much you
can do about it.'

'I'm going to try.' There was grim determination in
her manner, and he begged anxiously,

'Don't do anything foolish. Look, we'll discuss it
more fully tonight.'

The opera! She'd forgotten all about their date tonight. Aloud she said, 'If you don't mind, I'd rather not
go. I have too much on my mind to be good company.'

'Nonsense. An evening out will——'

'No, Philip,' she refused gently, then firmly excused herself on the pretext of having other calls to make. She felt physically sick, and more than a little disillusioned. Now there was nothing else for it but to face the illustrious Mr Andretti, and she didn't hold out much hope there!

Once more she set the telephone dial spinning, and as soon as her employer answered she interrupted his smoothly-voiced 'Monsieur Claude' with the request for a few hours off, pleading a family crisis as the reason. Claude broke into voluble French for all of three minutes before calming sufficiently to continue in English. It took a further few minutes before he agreed, albeit reluctantly, and Sally hastened to assure him that she would be at work just as soon as she could.

It was almost nine o'clock when she left the apartment, femininely attired in a cool dress of patterned voile with shirring across the bodice, the material falling in layered tiers from the waist. Twin shoe-string straps tied over each shoulder, and she teamed elegant white high-heeled sandals with a shoulder-bag in matching white. Her hair swung loose, and a touch of lipstick and eyeshadow was her only artifice.

Andretti Associates were listed in the telephone directory as occupying a suite in one of the modern high-rise buildings in the inner city, and she experienced a sense of trepidation as she walked into the impressive foyer. Idly she scanned the directory plaque for the correct floor. There it was—the tenth.

The door of one of the elevators was about to close just as she approached it, and as she reached out to press the calling button the door sprang back.

Sally stepped inside, a few polite words of gratitude

on her lips, and then she froze. It wasn't possible! The sole occupant was none other than the hatefully cynical man responsible for changing her tyre the previous afternoon.

'Good morning.'

Sally acknowledged his greeting with a slight nod, and wished she could control the faint tinge of pink that coloured her cheeks. The panel with designated buttons for each respective floor was on his side of the elevator, and she gave a cool monosyllabic directive in response to his mockingly raised eyebrow.

The elevator's ascent was rapid, but even in those few seconds she was aware of his slow appreciative appraisal. She deliberately refrained from looking anywhere near him, and when the elevator came to an electronically-precise halt she moved through the open doors with her head held high.

Whoever he was, he succeeded in ruffling her composure, she reflected crossly. He was taller than she remembered, an inch or two over six foot, and his hair appeared darker out of the sunlight. She had a vivid recollection of dark brown eyes in a face that was arresting, its bone structure broad and well-defined.

Oh, for heaven's sake—this was ridiculous! She'd probably never see him again, and what's more, she didn't want to.

Stepping briskly along the corridor, she paused outside opaque-glass doors whose lettering proclaimed that Andretti Associates could be found within, and with some misgivings she entered the carpeted foyer and gave her name to the receptionist.

'I'm sorry, Miss Ballinger, but Mr Andretti is not available at the moment.'

'Then I shall wait until he is,' Sally responded calmly, and received a dubious glance.

'I doubt Mr Andretti can see you this morning,' the other girl informed. 'Would you care to make an appointment—perhaps tomorrow?'

Sally shook her head, her heart sinking. 'It has to be today,' she said purposefully. 'I'll wait.'

The telephone buzzed, and the receptionist took the call, transferred it, then returned her attention to Sally.

'If you'll wait until Mr Andretti's secretary is free, I'll check if there's any possibility of him seeing you today.'

Sally nodded, then moved towards an assortment of comfortable chairs, selected one and sat down, at the same time letting her eyes wander over the expensive appointments evident. Andretti Associates obviously didn't balk at providing comfort to the point of luxury for their clients and staff, she determined. There was an adequate supply of magazines available, from *Time* to *Punch*, numerous financial bulletins, and a selection of fashion magazines.

'Miss Ballinger, it appears Mr Andretti can fit you in this morning,' the receptionist informed her, and Sally detected a note of surprise in the girl's voice. 'If you'll follow me, I'll take you through, and Mr Andretti's secretary will call you from there.'

Well, this was a turn-up for the book, Sally decided as she was led through to an ante-room that was sumptuously furnished. How long she would have to wait wasn't divulged, but it was enough that she was able to see the exalted Mr Andretti at all.

Thirty minutes dragged by, followed by another thirty, and Sally picked up yet another magazine and leafed through its contents. At precisely midday, when she thought they had forgotten about her, the door opened and a mature, efficient-looking woman informed her that Mr Andretti would see her now.

At last! Sally stood to her feet and followed in the secretary's wake, coming to a halt as she paused beside an open door.

'Miss Ballinger, Mr Andretti.'

Sally stepped inside as the secretary withdrew, hearing the firm click of the door as it shut behind her, and with determined resolve she lifted her gaze towards the tall figure outlined against the window on the far side of the room. There was something about him that was vaguely familiar, and as he turned slowly round to face her she gave a startled gasp of recognition.

CHAPTER TWO

'*You!*' Sally cried in shocked disbelief as soon as she found her voice. Dear God, this had to be a bad dream! The man in the elevator and the head of Andretti Associates were one and the same.

'At the risk of sounding facetious—yes.' He regarded her with an unwavering stare that seemed to hold her transfixed for an interminable length of time, then he moved round to the front of the desk and leaned against it, bidding her silkily, 'Do sit down, Miss Ballinger.'

Her head lifted a fraction. 'I'd prefer to stand.'

'As you wish.' He gave a negligent shrug, and she met his gaze defiantly, hating the slow analytical appraisal he subjected her to in an obvious attempt to disconcert, making her feel hopelessly angry, and only the mission on hand forced her to affect a measure of politeness.

'So,' he drawled, 'you have been despatched as an emissary.'

'My father doesn't know I'm here,' she declared with a calm she was far from feeling. 'The idea to see you was entirely my own.'

'With what object in mind?'

He was deliberately playing with her—and deriving a certain enjoyment from doing so, she perceived. The knowledge lent an edge to her tongue.

'You know why I'm here. Must I grovel on my knees?'

His eyes darkened momentarily. 'As yet, you have not answered my question.'

Sally endeavoured to retain a sense of calm—difficult, when she longed to slap his arrogant face! 'My father suffers from a heart complaint,' she explained carefully. 'Nothing imminently serious, but stress and worry must be avoided if he's to enjoy reasonable health.'

With a calculated movement he turned slightly, extracting a thin cheroot from an ornately-carved box on his desk, then he removed the wrapper and placed the cheroot between his lips. A lighter flared, and he took several deep inhalations before he considered the cheroot to be drawing to his satisfaction.

'You are fully aware,' he began slowly, 'of your father's financial position?'

'I know he faces bankruptcy—yes.'

'And you think I can prevent that?'

'You could give him more time,' she cried out, severely tried. 'If you don't press for payment, he may be able to come to some arrangement whereby such a drastic step as bankruptcy can be avoided.'

'I have already been lenient regarding his outstanding arrears,' he informed her bluntly. 'And yet you ask that I cast aside a stringent code of business ethics.'

Sally was stung into retorting, 'I had hoped you might be human enough to show a little sympathy, but that would be asking too much, wouldn't it?'

'Contrary to your cherished hopes, Sally Ballinger,' he drawled, 'I am not a benevolent charity organisation.'

'Then why did you allow me to see you?' she cried angrily. 'With the protective screening system you employ, I would never have made it past your secretary unless you'd sanctioned it.'

He looked at her coolly, letting his gaze rove indolently over her expressive features, lingering on her mouth until she moved uncomfortably as resentment, embarrassment, and worse—awareness tingled tantalisingly along her nerve-ends.

'Yesterday you managed to intrigue me. Today when you stepped into the elevator requesting the same floor as the one containing my offices—' he paused fractionally to stub out the remains of his cheroot, 'it was simple enough to put through a call from the next floor to my secretary and determine whether a silvery-blonde, blue-eyed girl by the name of Sally Ballinger was waiting in my reception lounge.'

'You knew who I was all along?' she queried in scandalised tones, and saw him lift an eyebrow in quizzical amusement.

'I took note of your car registration number, and had it traced.'

'Of all the——' She was lost for words. '*Why?*'

'As I said, you succeeded in arousing my interest.'

'It was quite unintentional, I assure you!'

His eyes gleamed with unconcealed mockery, and he gave a deep, throaty laugh. 'How long is it since you left the schoolroom, *piccina*—two, three years?'

'I turned twenty-three several months ago,' she asserted scornfully.

'Ah—so old,' he mocked. 'The mind boggles to understand why you are still single.'

Sally had a desire to shock the sardonic cynicism from those dark eyes. Mustering every ounce of calm, she ventured sweetly, 'Perhaps I'm frigid. I'd much rather tie myself to an inanimate stove than become one man's intimate slave!'

'One can only conclude you to be an untutored innocent,' he alluded cynically, 'or venture that your tutors to date have been amateurs.'

A tiny shiver slid slowly down the length of her spine. That *he* was no amateur was obvious!

'Shocked into silence?'

'Of course not,' she denied crossly. 'I didn't exactly come down with the last shower of rain!'

Almost as if she hadn't spoken, he commanded softly, 'I would like you to dine with me this evening.'

It gave her immense pleasure to meet his dark sardonic gaze, and shake her head in refusal. No doubt he had any number of women eager for his invitation and more than willing to succumb to his slightest whim. Well, she wasn't one of them! 'I shan't waste any more of your valuable time, Mr Andretti,' she declared deliberately, standing to her feet. 'I'm already late for work.'

'You decline?'

'As much as it must surprise you—yes. I wouldn't accept an invitation from you if—if I were dying of hunger!'

The lean mouth twitched in silent humour. 'I would not relish seeing those delectable curves reduced to skeletal emaciation,' he drawled lazily. 'What if I insist?'

'This is a free country, Mr Andretti—and yours isn't by any means the first proposition I've had to fend off!'

One eyebrow quirked slightly and his lips twisted in a wry smile. 'Was that what I was doing? I distinctly remember asking you to dine—not join me in a game of seduction.'

'With you, one would invariably lead to the other!' Sally flung with marked asperity, and turning, she began walking towards the door. 'Don't bother to see me out.'

It seemed almost an anti-climax to step into the corridor, and she managed a slight smile in the general direction of his secretary as she hurried past the adjacent reception lounge.

In the elevator she gave way to an unreasonable resentment, and crashed her gears more than once during the short drive to the catering firm where she worked.

'Ah, you're back,' Claude greeted with relief as soon as Sally walked into the large kitchen. Saucepans stood simmering on several hotplates, and a delicious aroma permeated the air. Marie and Adèle were busily engrossed preparing vegetables at the work-bench, and Henri wielded a stainless-steel chopper as he dissected poultry.

'I'm sorry I'm late,' she apologised. 'But it was unavoidable.'

Claude waved a dismissing hand. 'We are managing.' He shrugged philosophically, then became businesslike. 'You have a private dinner for two this evening.'

Sally gave him her full attention. 'What does she want the menu to consist of?'

'She's a he, dear, and as to the menu, that's to be left to your discretion,' Claude told her with satisfaction. 'Quite an honour. We're often requested to offer suggestions, but rarely is the entire menu left open.'

'One of our satisfied clients, no doubt,' she declared with an impish smile, only to see Claude frown.

'No. This is something of a *coup* for us. An Italian businessman who is held very much in regard among the social élite.'

'An Italian menu?' Sally suggested tentatively, and Claude indicated his approval.

'You do a beautiful *lasagne al forno*, or perhaps *cannelloni ripieni*? with chicken *cacciatore* to follow?'

'And *zabaglione*,' she enthused, 'for dessert.'

Claude's Cordon Bleu dishes were priced *à la carte*, with the final preparations being completed by one of his assistant chefs and served to the guests in the client's home. When catering for six or more, he insisted upon a waiter or waitress, whichever the client preferred, to serve at the table. His reputation was *par excellence*, and his charges precluded all but the wealthy.

'Dinner is to be served at eight,' Claude elaborated, adding, 'The address is Vaucluse, and the client's name is Andretti—Luciano Andretti.'

It was too much of a coincidence for it not to be—'I don't believe it!' Sally burst out incredulously, and Claude shot her a furious glance.

'My dear, I have the order written down. It was phoned in only ten minutes ago, and as you were not specifically engaged for the evening, Christine confirmed the booking.' He looked at her dubiously. 'Am I to understand you are acquainted with Mr Andretti?'

'Yes!' she exclaimed forcefully, causing Claude to raise a querying eyebrow. 'And I don't like him at all!'

'He's a very influential man. To acquire his patronage is no mean accomplishment. You must go, of course.'

'I'd very much like to refuse,' she declared balefully.

'As an assistant chef, you are very good at your job. I can't allow you to let personalities cloud your professional perspective,' Claude stated decisively. 'If I conducted my business by accepting bookings merely from clients who had my liking, I'd be a pauper!'

Sally gave an expressive sigh. Claude was right, but it didn't make the evening's prospect any easier.

'As the dinner is for two, you'll handle it on your own,' he informed her evenly, and she grimaced.

Tonight was going to be an elaborate charade which she'd prefer to miss entirely. Damn Luciano Andretti! she cursed violently. He was doing this deliberately for some devious reason of his own.

At precisely six-thirty, Sally drew the pale blue van with 'Claude's Catering' discreetly lettered in white on its doors to a halt on the brick-tiled driveway of an attractive architecturally-designed white-plastered mansion built on three levels to blend against the natural contour of the sloping ground. Exclusive and rather grand, she perceived wryly as she slipped out from behind the wheel and began unloading the stainless-steel trolley containing all manner of saucepans, partly-prepared food and utensils, from the rear of the van.

Not even on her first solo assignment with 'Claude's' had she felt so nervous, and it was reflected anger that made her jab the doorbell with unnecessary force.

The door opened almost immediately to reveal a short man of middle years with a polite smile of enquiry creasing his prominently-Roman features.

'I'm from "Claude's",' Sally informed him, proffering the personalised card she carried, and at once the man's expression lightened in comprehension.

'Ah, *sì*. Please come in.' He moved aside and gestured that he would assist with the trolley. 'Signor Andretti is expecting you.'

Is he indeed! She muttered beneath her breath. 'If you will show me where the kitchen is situated?' she queried aloud.

'Of course, *signorina*. Please follow me.' He proceeded to lead the way across the marble-tiled entrance towards an imposing flight of stairs leading to an upper floor.

There were expensive prints on the cream sculpture-plastered walls, an occasional inset containing valuable pieces of porcelain and Venetian glass, and as they reached the head of the staircase Sally had to concede that it was a beautifully-appointed home.

From the long hallway she glimpsed a spacious, luxuriously-furnished lounge, and an elegant dining-room. Deep-piled sage-green carpet sank softly beneath her feet, and the kitchen when she reached it was modern with up-to-date electrical appliances—the latest design in wall-ovens, she noted, as the man-servant began opening cupboards and drawers.

'Everything you need is here,' he assured her. 'If you will come with me, I will show you where everything is kept for the setting of the table.'

The dining-room was large, and along one wall and occupying its entire length was a vast mahogany side-board, containing at first glance sufficient glassware, dinner services and cutlery to cater for a large number of guests. Drawers revealed table-linen and napkins aplenty. The table was rectangular in shape, and like the sideboard, mahogany.

Back in the kitchen, Sally began taking utensils and saucepans from the trolley, checking each item off from the list she'd placed on top of the work-bench. How she wished she had had the courage to prepare an Indian curry so hot that the arrogant *signore* would positively gasp at the assault to his tastebuds!

'Good evening.'

Talk of the devil! Sally swung round, startled, at the sound of the cynical drawl. He had entered the kitchen as silently as a cat and was standing a few feet distant, his eyes dark and sharply analytical as they surveyed her.

'Good evening.' Her voice was a point above an arctic zero.

The manservant began a conversation in rapid Italian, and lapsed into English several seconds later to bid them both goodnight.

'Curious?' her adversary queried sardonically. 'Carlo made the observation that if you cook as well as you look, he envies me the meal.'

'If I were not representing "Claude's", the temptation to serve you toadstools in arsenic sauce would be almost too much to resist,' Sally declared with scathing sarcasm, and was stirred to unreasonable anger as he smiled with genuine amusement.

'A Lucrezia Borgia? I doubt you could, Sally Ballinger,' he mocked. 'You are all honey, with just sufficient spice to make things interesting.'

'Save your breath, *signore*,' she directed witheringly. 'I'm only the hired help—you can practise your so-called charms on your unenviable dinner date. Quite frankly, I'm singularly unimpressed.'

'*Signore?*' he queried with mocking emphasis. 'I much prefer Luke—the English equivalent of my given name, Luciano.'

'I came here to work, not to make conversation,' she stated, blandly ignoring him as she deftly removed lids from containers. 'I'm sure you don't want dinner to be late.'

His laugh was openly sardonic, and it only served to infuriate her further. She clenched her hands in silent enmity as the door closed behind him—how she'd like to burn each course to an unpalatable offering!

Immersed with preparations, she was oblivious to any sounds outside the kitchen, and it was only when she entered the dining-room to set the table that she gave further thought to Luke Andretti's guest. Undoubtedly she—and it had to be a woman—was sipping excellent sherry in the lounge with her host and indulging in witty conversation.

The dining-room table seemed rather long to seat the host and his guest at each end, and Sally chose the centre, placing an elegant silver candelabrum at either side of the table setting, with a single orchid beside each for decoration. She stood back to admire the setting, pleased with the way the candles in their silver stands balanced the length of the table. The dinner-service of bone china was quite plain, and was complemented by the silver cutlery gleaming beneath the subdued lighting. Delicately-stemmed crystal goblets sparkled with an almost diamond brilliance from their many-faceted patterns.

At precisely five minutes to eight, Sally took two bottles of wine from the refrigerator and set them on the table. She put the finishing touches to the serving dishes, then checked her wristwatch. Eight o'clock, exactly. Should she ask if dinner should be held back? She was about to step forward with the intention of consulting the host, when the kitchen door opened.

Luke Andretti looked vaguely piratical and dynamically masculine, having exchanged the sober business suit for casual dark trousers. A matching silk shirt of dark brown masked a firmly-muscled chest and broad shoulders, and his shirt-sleeves were turned back at the cuff. Half of the buttons down the front of his shirt had been left undone, revealing a deep vee of crisp dark hairs curling over darkly-tanned skin.

'If your guest is late, I can delay things for up to twenty minutes,' Sally began, deliberately aiming her gaze two inches to the left of him.

'My guest has been here for some time,' he informed her dryly, his dark eyes sweeping with slow indolence over her slim figure attired in its attractive pale blue uniform.

'In that case, I shall serve the starter.'

Luke Andretti nodded slowly, then turned and preceded her from the kitchen.

On reaching the dining-room, she was startled to see that it was empty, and she glanced round clearly puzzled.

'Take a seat, Sally Ballinger,' he bade mockingly, pulling out a chair, and at once she spluttered into indignant speech.

'If this is your idea of a joke——' she placed the dish on to the table—the temptation to throw it at him was very great. 'Why?' she questioned coldly. 'It must be patently obvious that I dislike you. Just what is it you want of me?' Her eyes sparked furiously alive. 'I can't believe it's merely my company for dinner—I'm not that gullible.'

'Sit down,' he directed smoothly. 'It would be a shame to spoil the excellent meal you have prepared.'

Sally felt the rage within her well up until it was ready to ignite. 'Eat it on your own, Mr Andretti. Nothing could persuade me to stay.'

His eyes held hers, dark and incredibly dangerous as he moved towards her. 'Perhaps you would prefer it if I lodged a complaint with your employer?' His voice held the threat to do exactly that, and she suppressed a slight shiver.

'You brought me here under false pretences,' she accused bleakly. 'I imagine you think you're very clever at having turned my refusal to dine with you into an obligatory acceptance. Forgive me if I decry your devious method!'

'If you do not sit down,' Luke Andretti told her ominously, 'I will surely lose what little patience I have left.'

Defeated, Sally subsided into the chair he held out

for her, and she eyed him warily as he moved round the table and began uncorking the wine. He filled her glass, then his own, before raising it to his lips.

'*Salute*,' he bade mockingly, and she deliberately left her glass untouched.

Conversationwise, the meal was a disaster. From the start Sally had been determined to treat Luke Andretti with an icy silence, but he forestalled any satisfaction she might have derived from such an exercise by not uttering so much as a word. Consequently, she felt close to boiling point by the time she retired to the kitchen to serve coffee, and while it was percolating she loaded the automatic dishwasher and set it in motion. With the ease of long practice she placed all of 'Claude's' saucepans and utensils back into the trolley in readiness for the moment when she could depart, cleaned down the work-bench, then set a tray with cups and saucers, sugar bowl, milk and cream.

When the coffee was ready, she poured it into two cups and carried the tray through to the dining-room.

'We will have it in the lounge,' Luke Andretti said smoothly, taking the tray from her nerveless hands.

She followed his broad back down the hallway, and entered the large, spacious lounge with a feeling of distinct unease.

The lighting was subdued, there were faint melodic strains emitting from concealed speakers, and it fairly screamed of a setting for seduction—hers! The strange air of foreboding became almost a tangible thing, threatening her composure in a way that was inexplicable.

Sally took the cup and saucer he handed her with hands that shook slightly, and she declined sugar and cream. Selecting a single armchair as far away from him as possible, she sipped the scalding liquid with more haste than care, and when the cup was empty she stood to her feet.

'So anxious to be gone?'

She drew a deep breath in an attempt to ignore the waves of panic creating havoc with her equilibrium. 'I've carried out my obligations for the evening,' she said evenly. 'There's no reason for me to stay.'

'Not even if I provide one?'

Blind anger prevailed at that thinly-veiled innuendo, and Sally erupted into incautious speech. 'What do you expect me to do? Offer myself in sexual gratification to plead my father's case?' Her eyes were alive with sparkling fury as she rounded on him. 'I wouldn't stoop that low—and especially not with you!' She lifted her chin defiantly, uncaring of the words she was about to utter. 'What will you do now—employ some devious Mafioso tactics to deprive my father of money he doesn't have? Rough him up a little—break a few bones? Even frighten him into an early grave?'

Slowly he rose to his feet, and there was a glimpse of terrible anger in the depths of those dark eyes that sent shivers of apprehension down Sally's spine.

'*Dio ch' aiuti!*' The oath was a husky growl. 'There is not a man alive I would permit to insult me in such a manner! You should thank every patron Saint ever consecrated that you were born a woman—otherwise I would thrash you to within an inch of your life!'

'If you so much as touch me, I'll scream,' she determined fiercely, and he uttered a harsh laugh.

'Who would hear you?'

Sally felt a momentary clutch of fear, and eyed the objects on a nearby cabinet with the intention of discovering a suitable weapon should she need it, then calculated the distance to the door.

'You would never make it,' he drawled, then swore

savagely. 'Cristo! It does not pay to blindly accuse a man of associating with the Mafioso merely because of his Italian heritage.' His eyes hardened until his expression became something frightening to behold. 'How highly do you value your father's peace of mind, Sally Ballinger?'

She swallowed painfully, for there was a lump in her throat that felt the size of an egg. 'What do you mean?'

His eyes never left her face as he revealed in a voice that had become ominously quiet. 'I want a son. It is not feasible to have worked so hard and not leave the fruits of my labours to the seed of my body.' He made a slow sweeping appraisal, roving from the top of her head down to the tips of her toes, and back again. 'You are a beautiful young woman, Sally Ballinger. I have an inclination to make you my wife. That is the price you must pay if you want me to put your father's financial affairs in order.'

Sally met his gaze through a nightmarish shroud that threatened to engulf her. 'Wife?' she echoed with bitter emphasis. 'Marrying you would be akin to marrying the devil!'

One eyebrow arched quizzically. 'You think so? That, however, does not give me an answer.'

For a long moment she just looked at him, then she ventured slowly, 'How do I know that I can trust you to do as you say?'

'Can you afford not to?'

Innumerable seconds ticked soundlessly by, and it could have been a hundred, or even a thousand that passed before she gave a drawn-out sigh. 'I need time to think it over.'

'You have precisely five minutes.'

'So generous!' she reiterated fiercely. 'I have to

choose between two forms of torture, each equally ab-horrent, and I'm expected to decide in *five minutes*? You're not only ruthless—you're inhuman!'

Luke Andretti checked the dial of his wristwatch. 'Four minutes and twenty seconds.'

'What possible satisfaction can you hope to achieve from a marriage doomed in hell?' Her voice held an anguish that was very real.

'But I am *il diavolo*—the devil himself—am I not? You hinted as much—and as such, I cannot be but comfortable in the fiery surroundings you regard to be my natural habitat.'

'You'd consign me there, as well?'

His smile was totally without humour. 'It may not be as hellish as you imagine.'

'I *hate* you!' she flung violently, and he intoned with intended cynicism,

'Better that than declare a love that is false.'

'I'll fight you every inch of the way, Luke Andretti,' she vowed emphatically. 'It will be a stormy possession, I promise you.'

His expression held mocking amusement as he glanced down at her. 'And be unnecessarily hurt, *piccina*? Such a folly would be unwise.'

'But wisdom doesn't enter into it, does it?' she parried bitterly. 'And if you call me "little child" again, I shall hit you!'

'Be warned I may retaliate,' he cautioned sardonic-ally.

'I might have guessed you would resort to wife-beating,' Sally declared trenchantly, and was totally en-raged when he began to laugh.

'An old-fashioned spanking,' Luke Andretti drawled, 'is remarkably different from an undisciplined act of violence.'

'You don't say!' she exclaimed with intended sarcasm.

'You seem hell-bent on discovering it for yourself, first-hand.' He leaned forward and took her chin between thumb and forefinger. 'Take heed, Sally Ballinger—I do not suffer fools gladly.'

She fell silent, and suddenly the enormity of what she was getting herself into wearied her beyond measure. It was almost all she could do not to shake visibly, but she was determined not to give this inimical—*savage* that satisfaction.

'A licence should take only a matter of days. Our—union should be legalised by the end of the week.'

A derisory, barely-audible snort erupted from Sally's throat. 'Misalliance, don't you mean?'

'I am sure you will discover it has some compensations,' he drawled, and she looked at him silently for several seconds before saying hesitantly,

'My father——'

'You have my word that his finances will be put in order,' Luke Andretti interrupted dryly, and she caught the edge of her lip with her teeth in a worried gesture.

'I don't quite know how he's going to accept all this. No matter what I say——'

'He will add two and two, and come up with the correct answer.'

'If he thinks I've sacrificed myself,' she began bleakly, 'it will hardly add to his peace of mind!'

'Then it will be up to you to disprove his suspicions.'

Sally cast him a sceptical glance. 'How, exactly?'

Luke's expression became faintly cynical. 'It might help allay his fears if you were to pretend an affection for me,' he suggested, 'and vice-versa.'

Her cheeks tinged a delicate pink. 'It will be difficult enough for me to suffer your—embraces,' she asserted heatedly, 'without having to put up with you pawing me in public!'

'I have not had any—er—complaints to date,' he drawled with a meaure of amusement.

'Then I shall be the first,' Sally declared, shooting him a baleful glare.

'My dear girl,' he drawled lazily, 'I have not so much as kissed you yet—so how can you complain?'

'Oh, you're impossible!'

'Undoubtedly,' he agreed mockingly, and caught hold of her arm as she turned away from him. 'Not so fast, *piccina*. There are a few matters we must discuss before you leave.'

Sally glared at him. 'Such as?'

Luke's eyes narrowed slightly, and he drew her inexorably close until there was barely an inch separating them. 'Already in the space of a day you have dared more than is tolerable,' he warned. 'Continue baiting me, and you will find I will not wait until my ring is on your finger.'

His meaning was unmistakable, and Sally felt a clutch of fear. 'What is it you want to discuss?' she queried, unconsciously running the tip of her tongue over the edge of her lower lip in a gesture that was motivated by nervous tension. 'It's quite late,' she pointed out tentatively, wanting only to escape from this hateful man. 'I have to report for work early tomorrow morning.'

'That is one of the things we must talk about,' Luke evinced mildly. 'You will hand in your notice, and leave either tomorrow or Thursday. I do not require a working wife—although I daresay Carlo will be grateful to be relieved in the kitchen occasionally. Tell me tomorrow evening if you experience any difficulties with your employer and I will contact him myself.'

'Tomorrow evening?' she queried, puzzled.

His smile was faintly cynical. 'When did you expect to see me next—at the register office a few minutes prior to the marriage?'

Sally's eyes were eloquent mirrors reflecting her distaste, and she held her tongue with difficulty.

'It would be appropriate if we celebrated our—engagement by having dinner together,' he added dryly. 'It would also be an excellent opportunity for me to have a few words with your father. Although I shall of course delay settling any of his accounts until after the wedding.'

'Of course,' Sally couldn't help mimicking bitterly, and received a hard shake by way of punishment.

'I will see you to your vehicle,' he determined brusquely. 'Carlo will already have returned and despatched your equipment downstairs.'

Sally rubbed her arms, grimacing at the bruising numbness from his steely grip. The impulse to poke out her tongue as she followed him down the broad staircase was too great to resist, and the childish gesture afforded her a measure of satisfaction.

The trolley was standing near the front door, and she pushed it out on to the driveway, then wheeled it towards the van.

'You have the key?' Luke questioned, holding out his hand, and when she ignored him he caught hold of her arm. 'Sally—the key, if you please.'

'Your act of chivalry doesn't impress me,' she flung jerkily. 'And I don't need your help. I've loaded and unloaded this trolley so many times I've lost count of them!'

'You wish me to tip out the contents of your bag?' he queried silkily, and she stifled an angry retort.

'Oh, have it your way,' she tossed, thrusting the key-ring into his hand, and she stood by impatiently as he unlocked the rear doors. She was so angry she didn't bother to explain about the collapsible twin planks that slid out to enable easy loading, but with effortless ease he merely lifted the trolley into the van's rear, secured the holding brakes to keep it stationary, then closed and locked the doors.

Accepting the keys from his outstretched hand, she was about to slip into the front seat when he caught hold of her shoulders and turned her round before she had a chance to struggle.

A hard kiss crushed her mouth, then she was free, and the sound of his brief laugh echoed in her ears all the way home.

CHAPTER THREE

THE following day was fraught with several problems, the first being the displeasure Claude initially voiced at having to accept two days' notice. Although by mid-morning he had mellowed sufficiently to proffer his congratulations, adding the caution that he hoped Sally wasn't letting her heart rule her head.

'He is an impatient man, this *beau*, eh? Cannot he wait a few weeks? *Mon dieu*, even one would do.' Claude invariably lapsed into his native French when roused, adopting continental gesticulations with abandon.

'It's all arranged, Claude,' Sally declared with a calm she didn't feel. 'Luke Andretti is a hard man to dissuade once he's made up his mind.'

His expression registered a mixture of emotions, then he nodded, deep in thought as he went over the bookings for the following few days. 'Ah well, if you were ill, we would somehow manage. Doubtless we will manage the same. You realise you have landed a very big fish?' he essayed suddenly, and she tried to instil some humour into the light laugh that emerged from her lips.

'I didn't exactly bait the hook, Claude,' she assured him dryly, and he smiled.

'I shall make your wedding cake—a gift, of course,' he determined, and she felt overwhelmed at his generous gesture.

'Thank you, Claude.'

He brushed aside her gratitude by turning the con-

versation back to business, and Sally found herself
with a multitude of tasks to complete. There wasn't a
great deal of time in which to think, and perhaps that
was a good thing, for she was sure that if she had an
ounce of sense she would tell Luke Andretti to go to
hell, and take the consequences.

By eleven o'clock 'Claude's' was a hive of activity,
and when, half an hour later, it was discovered that
one of the kitchen staff and a waitress had reported off
sick, the work-load on each of the staff present increased almost two-fold. Sally began to wish for two
pairs of hands, and Marie, one of the new waitresses
with less than two weeks' experience, was a bundle
of nerves.

'You, Sally,' Claude instructed wearily, 'will have to
serve the tables with Marie. Sophie, also. There is no
other way if we are to cope with any sort of *éclat*.
Georges will assist me in the kitchen.'

The occasion was a businessmen's luncheon held in
honour of a visiting dignitary, and there were to be
thirty guests in all. Expected to last three hours, it
began with canapés and champagne at midday, and
was to work its way through four courses, finishing
with coffee.

Sally circulated the lounge proffering the tray of
canapés, her face a polite smiling mask—although the
pose almost slipped when she recognised a familiar
profile in a group of five on the far side of the room.
Darn it, she cursed silently—of all the rotten luck!

Fortunately Sophie had already passed Luke Andretti's particular group, and Sally was able to keep
at a respectable distance. However, in the dining-room
she was not so fortunate, for he was seated near the
end of her allotted section of the table. Consequently,
she was forced to serve him, and his acknowledgment

of her presence was cordially pleasant, evoking the interest of more than two of his companions.

Thereafter she became conscious of his eyes frequently observing her actions, so that she felt her fingers become thumbs, and curbing an inner anger she daren't give vent to, she began longing for the ensuing few hours to pass swiftly. It was ridiculous to feel like a fly caught in the spider's web—but she did.

It didn't help when Marie positively swooned over Sally's good luck at having such an attractive-looking man among those she was serving.

'I adore Latin men, don't you? He has to be Latin!' the younger girl enthused. 'So dark and vital, with that brooding quality—one can't be sure whether it'll erupt as passion or temper!' She gave a laugh, then voiced speculatively, 'Actually, I think he looks a bit dangerous.'

'He sends chills down my spine,' Sally retorted with unveiled sarcasm, and Marie turned from her task of placing spoons into serving dishes.

'I've been watching him, and for what it's worth—I think he has his eye on you.'

'Well, he can just take it off,' Sally voiced with unnecessary vehemence, so that the other girl looked positively startled. Really, in a moment she'd scream!

'You don't like him?'

'I'm really much too busy to form an opinion,' Sally responded, placing two of the serving dishes on to a tray.

The remainder of the afternoon flew with a swiftness that was hardly credible, and it was almost six o'clock when Sally let herself into the apartment. She felt hot and decidedly jaded. In an hour Luke Andretti would arrive, and she had to shower, cook something for her father's evening meal, get ready, *and* attempt to explain her forthcoming marriage.

She shut the door behind her, then moved towards the lounge, hearing as she did so her father's voice raised in anger. She was momentarily nonplussed, for rarely had she had occasion to hear him so much as raise his voice to anyone, least of all to her, but it was obvious he was handling a very irate conversation with someone on the other end of the telephone. Unable to hear clearly, she stood transfixed at the sheer desperation in his voice, and unwilling to be an eavesdropper, she backtracked a few steps and made the pretence of noisily shutting the apartment door.

'Hi—I'm home!' she called out with as much gaiety as she could muster, and at once her father's voice dropped to an inaudible murmur.

Idly, she sifted through the mail resting on the dining-room sideboard, determining that none were addressed to her, although there were three separate messages penned in her father's scrawl informing her that Philip had called requesting she ring back the moment she arrived home.

Curious, she went into the kitchen and took a jug of iced fruit juice from the refrigerator, filled a tall glass, then sipped the contents. Joe entered the room when she had consumed almost half of it, and his features were controlled into a relaxed smile.

'You're earlier than I expected,' he observed, and Sally cast him a speculative look that searched for and found nothing untoward in his expression.

'I know,' she sighed, then grimaced a little. 'The luncheon was successful, but what a behind-the-scenes fiasco! Adèle didn't show up, Spiros rang in at the eleventh hour unable to make it, and I had to be both waitress and chef's assistant.'

'Rough,' Joe sympathised. 'There's some steak—

let's have it grilled, with a salad. It's almost too hot to think of eating.'

Well, there was no time like the present, Sally decided. 'I'll be dining out tonight. You don't mind, do you?'

'Of course not. A date with Philip? He rang, by the way,' he told her with a slight smile. 'Very keen, that young man.'

'My date isn't with Philip, Daddy.' Dear heaven, this was getting difficult. 'Look, I must rush if I'm to be ready in time. I'll slip under the shower, then while I'm grilling your steak you can bring your sherry into the kitchen and I'll tell you all about it. Okay?' She smiled, then leaned forward and kissed his cheek, escaping before he had a chance to voice his surprise.

After a shower, Sally slipped into fresh underwear, then pulled on a robe and returned to the kitchen with an air of fatalism.

'Thought I'd save you some time,' said Joe as he slid the meat beneath the griller. 'I've already tossed the salad.' He held out a glass containing clear amber liquid, then as the telephone began to ring insistently, he crossed the room and picked up the receiver.

'Philip,' he revealed quizzically, and her heart sank.

'I'll take it in the study.' Even a few minutes' reprieve were not to be sniffed at, and Sally clutched at them like a drowning man.

With the study door closed carefully behind her, she moved across to the desk and picked up the receiver.

'Sally?' Philip rushed on before she had a chance to say so much as a word. 'I've been worried about you. Why haven't you answered my calls?'

'I've only been home a short while,' she explained. 'I intended ringing you as soon as I'd fixed dinner.'

'How did you get on yesterday?' His voice crackled

with anxiety, and Sally tried to inject some enthusiasm into her response.

'The problem has been solved, Philip.'

'What do you mean? You've managed to raise some money?'

'Yes,' she answered slowly, reluctant to parry the barrage of questions that would inevitably follow.

'All of it?' The voice on the other end came through sharp and faintly incredulous, and she gave a mono-syllabic answer. 'I find that hard to believe,' he ex-postulated with obvious perplexity. 'How?'

'I don't believe that's any of your business,' she man-aged calmly, and he made a stifled, inarticulate re-joinder before declaring decisively,

'I'll come round and we'll talk about it.'

Sally made an instant and emphatic demur. 'That's quite unnecessary, Philip. Besides, I already have a date this evening.'

There was silence for a few seconds. 'Two years, Sally? And you can switch off, just like that?'

I was never at any time switched on, she thought sadly. Aloud, she chose her words with care. 'I begged you for help, Philip, and you offered several reasons as to why you had to refuse,' she said slowly. 'I had little choice but to appeal to the man I considered my last resort.'

'I'm coming to see you—now.'

'Don't,' she protested quickly. 'It wouldn't be pleas-ant for either of us, and my father would be unneces-sarily upset.'

'God!' he uttered desperately. 'Two *years* I've part-nered you to all the best places—and got nothing but a few cool kisses in return. It's a well-known fact that your father is in over his neck to Andretti. I suppose you've sold yourself to *him*, Sally, for the——'

Sickened, she replaced the receiver, then ran shaky fingers through her hair. The thought of having to face her father, and *smile*, was going to prove no mean acting feat!

Joe was seated at the table when she entered the dining-room, and he was just starting his meal. He looked up, giving a slightly puzzled laugh as he saw his daughter swallow the entire contents of her glass in one deep mouthful.

'You obviously needed that—but really, my dear! That's sacrilege—sherry should be sipped, not gulped.'

'Exit Philip—enter Luke,' Sally declared with an attempt at the banal. If she wasn't blasée about the whole thing, she'd burst into hysterical tears!

'Luke?'

'Luciano Andretti,' she said firmly, and saw her father register a gamut of emotions—surprise, shock, disbelief, and lastly concern.

'What have you done, Sally?' he queried anxiously, and she subsided into the nearest chair to sit facing him.

'Luke and I are going to be married,' she said carefully, and at once he began to splutter incredulously.

'Sally, I demand to know——' He faltered on hearing a peremptory rap at the front door, and Sally seized the opportunity to escape.

Reaching the door, she pulled it open to find Luke Andretti's tall frame filling the doorway, and at the same time heard her father's angry gasp from behind. Afterwards, she couldn't for the life of her think what made her do what she did. It was a moment of pure insanity, and she reacted accordingly.

'Why, darling, you're early!' she greeted Luke enthusiastically, and stepping close she stood on tiptoe, then wound her arms round his neck and kissed him.

Well, that was how it began, and Luke, to give him credit, didn't turn a hair or hesitate so much as a fraction of a second. He kissed her back—thoroughly, his arms curving over her slim form, holding her close with as much familiarity as if they'd embraced her a hundred times.

When he released her, Sally turned slowly round to face her father with pink-tinged cheeks, parted lips, and a sparkle in her eyes that only she knew to be anger.

'I think we owe you an explanation,' Luke offered smoothly as he stepped through the doorway and firmly shut the door.

Sally experienced a strange feeling of unreality, almost as if the room and everyone in it was part of some strange dream from which she would eventually awaken. She didn't even resist when Luke curved an arm about her waist, and she found herself murmuring, 'I tried to tell him——'

'I am sure you did, *cara*,' Luke drawled with seeming fondness. 'But now that I am here, I shall do it for you.' He leant down and brushed his lips across her forehead, then straightened and shot an amused glance towards her father. 'I have to admit to being a little bemused by it all myself.'

He was convincing, Sally had to admit. With a few apparently genuine words, he managed to dispel most of Joe's suspicions. It would be impossible to state categorically that he dispelled them *all*, but her father appeared willing to accept things at face value.

'And now, *amante*,' Luke directed gently, 'go and change, while I talk with your father, hmm?'

Sally didn't need second bidding, and she escaped from his side with alacrity. Only when she was in the safety of her own room did she sink down on to the bed and bury her head into the pillow in despair.

How long she remained there, she had no recollection, for time became a suspended element, and it could have been five or thirty minutes before a muted knock on the bedroom door roused her sufficiently to slip off the bed.

'Tell Luke I won't be long,' she called in a falsely-bright voice. 'I——' she faltered, and when the door opened she turned quickly away.

At the sound of the closing door, she gave a heartfelt sigh of relief that was shortlived as hard hands caught hold of her shoulders and swung her round.

'*Cristo!*' Luke swore softly as his eyes raked her face. 'What in the name of heaven happened before I arrived?'

'Nothing,' she answered shakily. 'I expected an adverse reaction from my father, and you arrived in the middle of it.' She raised distraught eyes to his. 'You can't come into my bedroom,' she protested, and he smiled rather grimly.

'If it worries your outraged sensibilities I'll open the door just as soon as you have got rid of that robe and slipped into an evening gown.'

Her eyebrows rose incredulously. 'You can't stay here while I change,' she charged angrily.

'Why? You are not entirely bare beneath that silky thing,' he drawled musingly. 'And I will vouch that your underwear covers you adequately—more so than that delightfully brief bikini of the other day.'

'Go away!' Her voice was a furious whisper, and his expression became sardonic.

'Get changed, Sally, or I will be tempted to give you a helping hand.' Without a further word he crossed to the wardrobe and flung open the door, sliding hangers this way and that as he made a cursory inspection before extracting a gown of blue silk-knit jersey. 'Wear this,' he commanded. 'It matches your eyes.'

She faced him mutinously, tears of frustration shimmering in her eyes, and as he took a step towards her she snatched the gown from his hands and turned away. 'You're a brute,' she accused, hating him, 'and a bully!' The robe slipped off her shoulders, and she slid the gown over her head, pulling it down with quick angry movements. Her hand went to fasten the zip at the back, only to encounter his fingers on the fastener, and she emitted a gasp of pure rage.

'Easy, *piccina*,' Luke warned. 'You had better recall a captivating smile, otherwise that embrace we convincingly shared and my carefully worded reassurances will all be for nothing.'

Sally knew he was right, but the knowledge did little to dampen her anger. She began applying make-up with carefully controlled speed, highlighting her eyes with eye-shadow and mascara, then added a touch of colour to her lips. Her brush dragged through her hair, assaulting her scalp until it tingled.

'Leave it loose,' Luke bade quietly, and she directed him a wrathful glance before crossing to the wardrobe to extract a pair of evening sandals.

'I'm ready.'

His eyes slid over her, swift and analytical. 'Looking at you, no one would believe the result was achieved in less than ten minutes. We will bid your father goodnight, then leave.' His expression hardened slightly as he glimpsed the soft trembling of her lips. 'You can resort to feminine hysterics once we are safely downstairs. Now, smile,' he commanded softly, and taking hold of her arm he swung open the door.

Somewhere along the hallway Sally mustered a measure of control, and when they entered the lounge seconds later, she was able to manage a slight smile. If awards were being given, she undoubtedly deserved an Oscar!

''Bye, Daddy.' She leaned forward and kissed his cheek. 'Wake me before you leave for work in the morning. We'll have a leisurely breakfast together, and talk.'

She was vaguely aware of Luke murmuring something to Joe, then they were out of the apartment and she was being led swiftly down the stairs. The Alfa-Romeo was parked in the courtyard, and she stood in silence while Luke unlocked the passenger door.

When she was safely seated he closed the door with a decisive snap, then moved round to slip in behind the wheel. He didn't start the engine at once, and leaning close he reached into the glovebox and took out a small jeweller's box.

'Your hand, if you please,' he ordered quietly, and when she refused to comply he reached out and grasped her wrist, straightening her fingers so that he could slip the ring he extracted on to her finger.

'I don't want a ring,' Sally flung wretchedly, not even wanting to glance at it, and his eyes narrowed.

'It is too late to think of changing your mind.'

'Dear God, I have to be mad!' she uttered piously.

'Without my assistance,' Luke began hardily, 'your father will be forced to give up his apartment, his car.' He went on relentlessly, 'Socially, he will become an outcast—ostracised by those who, until now, have been so-called friends.'

Sally shuddered from the cruel picture he painted. 'You will play Shylock,' she voiced slowly, 'if I provide the pound of flesh.' She met his gaze defiantly in the encroaching dusk. 'Be very sure, Luke Andretti, that if it were not for my father, I would take great pleasure in telling you to go to hell!'

'Are you usually so objectionable with all members of the male sex?'

Hating his amused cynicism, she resorted to rudeness. 'Only with you.'

'One is wont to wonder why,' he mused dryly.

'Wonder as much as you like!' she retorted, and was infuriated when he laughed.

'My, my,' Luke drawled. 'You are a prickly young woman—a veritable *porcospino*, in fact.'

'And you're a *devil*!'

'So you seem fond of telling me.' He reached out a hand and switched on the ignition. 'Perhaps a meal will improve your disposition.'

For a moment she felt oddly penitent. Whatever manner of man he was, he had kept his side of the bargain—smoothing the way with her father, and even going so far as to present her with an engagement ring for appearances' sake.

'The past few days haven't been very easy,' Sally offered slowly as they neared the inner city. 'You always seem to have the upper hand.'

Luke's slight smile was without mockery. 'And that irks you, does it not?'

'Unbearably,' she admitted wryly. 'I want to scream and rage against fate for being so unkind.'

'But mostly against me,' he declared dryly, 'for daring to take fate by the tail and turn it to my advantage.'

'Yes.'

The remainder of the drive was completed in silence, and in the restaurant Sally sipped champagne and allowed Luke to order the meal, hardly caring what she ate.

'The food is not to your liking?'

Sally looked up and met his faintly raised eyebrow.

'I'm not very hungry,' she declared quietly.

'If I ask you to dance, you will undoubtedly decline,' he drawled sardonically, and a perverse little imp caused her to raise her head in cool defiance.

'Not at all—I love to dance. Unless——' she paused, unable to resist adding, 'this music is too modern for you?'

His eyes lit with a devilish gleam. 'At thirty-seven, I am scarcely in my dotage. I manage a mean tango, and I have been known to attempt the hustle.'

'Really?' Sally queried politely as she preceded him on to the floor.

Much to her surprise he was familiar with most of the latest steps, executing them with a natural flair and without any sense of exhibitionism, and after a while she forgot to consider him an enemy and began to enjoy herself.

When the tempo changed she stopped, and she would have turned back towards their table had Luke not grasped hold of her arm. She looked at him then, and saw the faint mockery evident in those dark eyes, and before she could escape he pulled her into his arms to hold her a good deal closer than was strictly conventional. Her hand felt ridiculously small in his, and she was aware of a set of powerful shoulders, a hidden strength in the arms that lightly held her. For some strange reason her pulse quickened, and she found herself swallowing nervously. This was ridiculous, for she didn't even like the man!

Somehow she expected him to speak—something wholly cynical, or indulge in sophisticated patter to fill the silence between them. But when he led her back to their table ten minutes later they hadn't exchanged so much as a word.

Sally resumed her seat, declined dessert, electing

to sip another glass of champagne and let her gaze wander idly over the patrons frequenting this exclusive restaurant. Her eyes widened a little as they rested on Chantrelle Bakersfield, then flew open as she glimpsed her companion. Philip! And they were slowly coming this way, weaving between the tables as they followed the head waiter. As they drew close, Sally almost closed her eyes in the fervent hope they wouldn't catch sight of her, but there was no such luck. However, it was Luke who first gained recognition, and the sound of Chantrelle's tinkling laugh attached to his name almost made Sally grind her teeth.

'Hello, you elusive man,' Chantrelle greeted him effusively. 'You haven't accepted one of my invitations these past few weeks.' She still had her back to Sally, but Philip had seen her and was glowering darkly.

'I have had little spare time,' Luke intimated smoothly, and Chantrelle shook her head meaningfully.

'I can see that, darling.' Her laugh was incredibly droll. 'Perhaps next week?' Then she turned, clearly with the intention of assessing the competition, and her slight gasp of surprise was quite genuine. 'Good heavens, Sally Ballinger!'

'Chantrelle,' Sally managed evenly, then let her greeting include the man at Chantrelle's side. 'Philip.'

'Champagne? Why, darling,' Chantrelle pouted engagingly as she returned her attention to Luke, 'are you celebrating another merger or something?'

Sally glimpsed Luke's mocking smile. 'You could say that,' he returned obliquely, and Chantrelle leaned forward, placing a hand on his arm.

'You choose to celebrate alone?'

'Sally and I did not think it necessary to include anyone else.'

'Sally?' She obviously didn't deserve mention. 'Does her presence have any significance?'

In a moment I'll scream, Sally decided, as Luke met the fighting gleam darkening her eyes and noted the twin flags of colour high on each cheek. He reached out and caught hold of her hand, deliberately spreading her fingers between his own, and the smile he gave her was shockingly intimate.

'Definitely,' he announced softly. 'Congratulations are in order—I am renouncing bachelorhood in favour of marriage.'

'You're *engaged*?' Chantrelle's voice rose an octave. 'To each other?'

Luke agreed, and his eyes gleamed wickedly as he took in Sally's angry blush.

'And the wedding?' Chantrelle persisted impolitely. 'It will take place next year, I presume?'

'The day after tomorrow,' Luke declared silkily, not taking his eyes from Sally's face for a second. 'We decided we could not wait—is that not so, *cara*?' he queried gently, and Sally made a strangled mono-syllabic reply that neither confirmed nor denied.

Chantrelle's eyes narrowed. 'Sally is a dark horse,' she stated with unveiled sarcasm. 'Up until a few days ago Philip understood he was to be the lucky man. Shame on you, Sally, for leading him on!'

'I never at any time led Philip on,' Sally responded evenly. 'If he imagined otherwise, then the fault is his, not mine.'

'Really?' Chantrelle widened her eyes with deliberate guile. 'Why, the dear boy is positively heartbroken at the way you've thrown him over!'

Sally could feel Luke's eyes lazily appraising her, and she seethed inwardly. 'No doubt he'll revive rapidly in your company, Chantrelle,' she managed with deliberate sweetness, and the other girl laughed.

'I certainly shan't hold him at arm's length, darling. Although I'm very sore at you for snaring this gorgeous man'—she indicated Luke with a playful finger tip, 'right from beneath my nose. I rather had my eye on him.'

'Obviously that wasn't enough.' Sally caught the gleam in Luke's eye and could cheerfully have hit him. He was regarding both girls with cynical amusement, and gave every appearance of enjoying their exchange.

'We'll move on to our table,' Chantrelle declared, and she shot Luke a speculative glance. 'Sally isn't really a worthy enough—partner for you. However, if you're dissatisfied——' she allowed the words to trail off provocatively as she took Philip by the arm and led him away.

Sally picked up her glass with a hand that was visibly shaking, and took a too generous sip of the amber liquid. She coughed, and took a moment to regain her breath.

'More champagne?' Luke queried, and she shook her head.

'I'd like to go home, if you don't mind.'

His eyes swept her stormy features, and he smiled. 'You would be wise not to let that social butterfly upset you.'

'Forgive me if I don't possess your cynicism!'

'One does not achieve success without becoming aware of the frailties of human nature,' he informed her dryly.

'If you won't take me home, I'll catch a taxi,' Sally determined stoically as she stood to her feet. To stay here another minute was impossible. Her emotions were a chaotic mixture of outrage and sheer anger. She

began moving away, uncaring whether he followed her
or not.

On reaching the foyer she swept past the cashier and
ran quickly down the stairs to street level. As luck
would have it a cruising taxi caught her attention and
without hesitation she hailed it.

As it slowed and came to a halt at the edge of the
kerb she was about to open the rear door when her arm
was caught from behind.

'I think not,' Luke murmured softly, and moving
close to the waiting taxi he bent low and dismissed the
driver.

There was an answering mutter of words, then Luke
uttered a laugh and responded in swift, incomprehen-
sible Italian. In a few short seconds the taxi slid away
into the stream of traffic.

'Why did you do that?' Sally burst out furiously.
'What did you say to him?'

His smile was wholly cynical. 'I simply explained
that your gesture of independence was motivated by
a lovers' tiff,' he intimated sardonically as he began
leading her along the pavement. 'I have no intention
of allowing you to find your own way home.'

'You're detestable!'

'Eventually you must run out of adjectives,' he declared dryly, and she gave a cry of anger as each suc-
cessive attempt she made to escape from his steely grip
proved fruitless.

'*And* remarkably thick-skinned,' she added for good
measure, and saw his lips twist slightly in humour as
he paused beside the Alfa-Romeo and unlocked the
passenger door.

'Get in, Sally,' he commanded, and she slid in, full
of resentment at his proprietorial tone. The door
snapped shut, and she watched him move round the car

to slip in behind the wheel.

'Our wedding will take place at one o'clock on Friday, followed by a luncheon at my home,' Luke told her as he set the car purring smoothly away from the city. 'Just your father and Carlo, of course, besides ourselves.'

'How nice,' Sally declared with intended sarcasm. 'I hope the ceremony is to be conducted in the register office. I don't intend wearing traditional bridal regalia, and to have the nuptials receive a sacred blessing would be incredibly ludicrous.'

'The register office,' Luke confirmed dryly. 'After which we will leave for the airport and catch the late afternoon flight to Auckland.'

'Why New Zealand?' she queried bleakly. 'Isn't embarking on a so-called honeymoon taking things a little too far?'

'I thought a few days on our own,' he explained silkily, and Sally uttered a harsh laugh.

'Somewhere far enough away so that I can't escape home to Daddy?'

'I would advise you not to concoct any schemes,' Luke warned dangerously. 'I am not without influence, and you would eventually be found.'

'To face a fate worse than death? There are laws to protect women from harassment.'

'What I had in mind was something infinitely more subtle.'

Sickened, she gazed sightlessly out of the side window, not wanting to pursue any futher conversation, and the remainder of the drive home was achieved in silence.

As soon as the car came to a halt in the courtyard outside her father's apartment block, Sally reached for the door-clasp, only to be forestalled by a hand on her arm.

'So anxious to be gone,' he mocked. 'Afraid I might ravish you, Sally Ballinger?'

'Not *before* the wedding,' she flung incautiously. 'Although doubtlessly you'll resort to force, even rape —afterwards!'

Luke uttered a few unintelligible oaths, and his grip on her arm tightened until she gasped with pain. 'You have the temerity of a hellcat,' he bit out harshly. 'I would advise you to curb your foolish tongue before I silence it.'

'Oh? And how do you propose to do that?'

There was a glimpse of terrible anger in those dark eyes, then she was half-lifted across the space between them to be held in an iron-like embrace, and there was no escape from the lips that descended on hers with deliberate intent.

His mouth bruised hers, the relentless pressure forcing her lips apart, and her entreaty to desist became an inaudible moan. Not content, he began a ravaging exploration that was nothing less than a total invasion of her shattered senses.

When at last he lifted his head and released her, she almost fell back into her seat, and she sat there unable to move, her eyes huge pools of darkened blue in a face that was pale beneath its tan. Of their own volition her hands crept up to cover her mouth, and she was conscious of their visible trembling. She desperately wanted to look away, but her eyes were riveted to his, almost as if they were held by a force stronger than her own.

'*Dio!*' Luke swore softly. 'Must you look at me like that? I only kissed you.'

'It feels as if you plundered my soul,' Sally faltered shakily.

'You provoked it.' His tone was harsh, and defeated, she turned away.

'If that—onslaught was intended to prove your superiority, then round one is undoubtedly yours,' she accorded wearily, and releasing the door-clasp she stepped out from the car. She was unaware that Luke followed her until his hand caught hold of her arm just as she was about to step through the apartment block's main entrance.

'I will see you safely upstairs,' he declared brusquely.

'There's no need to be so gallant—I'm quite able to take care of myself.'

He smiled slightly, but refrained from making any comment as he summoned the elevator.

Sally fought off a disturbing mixture of emotions that alternated between fear and awareness, sending prickles of apprehension tingling down the length of her spine. He wasn't a man she could successfully ignore, and never before had she encountered anyone quite like him.

'Your key?' Luke queried as they stepped out into the corridor, and she directed him a waspish look.

'Really—you can leave now.'

'When I have seen you into the apartment,' he responded unperturbed, and she gave an expressive sigh as she stood to one side while he fitted her key into the lock.

As the door swung open, she couldn't resist querying, 'Satisfied?'

'Not quite.'

She was too emotionally weary to struggle as he caught her close, and she closed her eyes in an effort to control the threatening tears welling up inside. They were a luxury she daren't indulge—at least, not yet. Later in the privacy of her room she could give way to a storm of angry weeping. Her lips trembled slightly beneath his, dreading a further assault, but it never came. Instead, his touch was little more than a light caress as his lips moved gently back and forth on hers, warm and insistently probing, before trailing up over her cheekbone to settle gently on each closed eyelid in turn.

'Carlo will drive both you and your father to the register office,' he intimated, setting her away from him. 'I will see you then. *Ciao, piccina.*'

Slowly Sally closed the door, switching off the light as she made her way towards her room. The entire day had been too fraught with various emotions for sleep to be an easy captive, despite an overwhelming weariness that seemed to seep into her very bones. Tomorrow involved a twelve-hour working day, her last at 'Claude's', and would preclude any shopping. There was nothing else for it but to make an early start on Friday morning. At least she'd be so busy she wouldn't have time to think!

CHAPTER FOUR

THE wedding ceremony had been brief and impersonal, the luncheon elaborate and superb—prepared, surprisingly, by Claude.

There was champagne, Dom Perignon, and the wedding cake was a two-tiered affair with intricately-patterned icing that it seemed a shame to desecrate. However, slice into it they did, and a small piece was solemnly sampled by each of them.

Sally had selected a two-piece ensemble of beige swiss jersey, comprising a blouson-styled jacket and a skirt that flared softly down to calf-length. Together with slender-heeled strappy shoes and a shoulder-bag in matching beige, she looked incredibly elegant and wraith-like.

Luke Andretti had chosen a superbly-tailored suit of dark brown, beneath which he wore a beige silk shirt and matching tie, appearing the sophisticated businessman he undoubtedly was.

To all outward appearances they seemed a well-matched pair, but Sally could only wonder that her father, Carlo, or even Claude for that matter, could possibly be taken in by any of it.

'We will need to leave soon.'

Sally looked up at the tall man by her side, and endeavoured a smile. 'Whenever you're ready.'

'Carlo has stowed our bags into the boot of the car,' Luke declared, flicking back the cuff of his jacket to ascertain the time, and Sally responded evenly,

'I'll slip into the kitchen and say goodbye to Claude.'

The trolley was loaded and the kitchen restored to an orderly state when she entered, and Claude gave her a wide grin.

'Ready to leave? So am I. Mr Andretti's manservant will attend to the lounge on his return.' He looked at her closely, observing, 'You look very pale—hardly the radiant bride, at all.'

Oh heavens, she'd have to perk up a bit! 'Nerves, Claude,' she dismissed lightly. 'I suppose every girl experiences a few doubts on her wedding day.'

'I'm sorry to lose you,' the Frenchman evinced sincerely. 'With your talent, I doubt you'll need my services in the future.'

She swallowed the slight lump in her throat, hesitating fractionally. 'I'd better go. The others are ready to leave.'

'Good luck, Sally.'

She smiled her thanks, then slipped out of the room and had almost reached the lounge when Luke stepped into the hallway, obviously with the intention of fetching her. His slightly raised eyebrow brought a faint flush to her cheeks, and she suffered his clasp on her arm downstairs to the car.

The drive to the airport was achieved in half an hour, and there was scarcely any time for more than a few interrupted snatches of conversation as Luke passed in their suitcases, then filled in the necessary forms for customs.

''Bye, honey,' Joe Ballinger bade, embracing his daughter warmly. 'I know you'll be happy. God bless.' He looked completely relaxed, and most of the tension that had added years on to his age had all but disappeared.

'I'll ring you when we get back,' was all Sally could find to say as the loud speaker announced their flight, instructing passengers to proceed through the departure lounge to Customs.

Then they were out of sight of the mingling crowd, and she felt oddly vulnerable—all too aware of having passed through a one-way door in more senses than one. The man at her side was now her husband, and that fact added a new dimension to their brief, stormy relationship.

Without conscious thought her eyes slid down to her hands, and as if to deliberately taunt her, a stray shaft of light effected a myriad prismatic scintillations from the magnificent diamond in its solitaire platinum setting adorning the third finger of her left hand. The wedding ring was platinum, its plainness relieved by several small diamonds inset into the wide band, and together their perfection brought a silent gasp of admiration to her lips. No less exquisite was the platinum wristwatch, its clockface encircled with diamonds, that Luke had given her less than an hour ago. She had been momentarily embarrassed, for she hadn't thought it necessary to give him anything.

Aboard the large DC-10 Sally moved down the aisle and took her seat nearest the window, thankful that this was not her first major flight. Two years previously she had crossed the Atlantic to spend a month's holiday with her mother in New York, and now she was able to present a reasonably relaxed façade during take-off and the jet's rapid ascent.

'Magazine?'

Sally cast a startled glance in the direction of that cynically-amused drawl. 'Thank you,' she accepted calmly, taking the gaily-printed periodical from Luke's hand. With outward casualness she flipped the pages, pretending interest.

The three hours' flying time seemed to be taken up

by the seemingly endless endeavours of the steward-esses to ply them with both food and drink. Conse-quently, by the time dinner was served, it was all she could do to sample a little from each course. Through-out, Luke set himself the task of being an urbane companion, keeping up an easy flow of conversation that was in direct antithesis to her rather monosyllabic replies.

The only part of the conversation that registered was that New Zealand observed daylight-saving during the summer months, which, with the two hours' time dif-ference between the two countries, would put their arrival time at approximately an hour and a half be-fore midnight. After clearing Customs and collecting the hired car, they would undoubtedly drive straight to their motel.

It all seemed to be happening too fast, Sally re-flected, reluctantly suffering Luke's light clasp on her elbow as he led her towards the large car parked in readiness beside the kerb. She felt she should be ex-cited at being in another country—enthusiastic, at least. Instead, there was no sense of having crossed an ocean or touching down on strange soil. There was nothing, only an impending sense of dread.

She was vaguely aware of Luke's voice informing her that their motel was situated in Parnell, an inner-city suburb, but she had no inclination to ask how far Par-nell was away from the airport, or how long it would take to get there.

As soon as the car was in motion she sat staring sightlessly ahead out the windscreen, consciously aware of every passing minute bringing her closer to the mo-ment when Luke would truly make her his wife. She suppressed a bitter laugh. Oh God, it was incredibly ironic that in this era of sexual freedom and the pill, she had stoically held on to her moral principles. Now she was irretrievably committed to a man whose sole purpose for marriage was to beget a son. There was not even the slightest measure of affection between them so that she might hope for a little tenderness in his lovemaking.

The street lights outside cast a white glow, illuminating the adjacent pavement in evenly-spaced patches, and there was little to be seen beyond the dark perimeter of shadow. An increasing flow of traffic and frequent computer-controlled intersections indicated that they were nearing the city itself, and within minutes the car deviated from the main road to come to a halt inside a large sweeping courtyard. At once Sally felt her stomach lurch into a series of painful somersaults, and only determined effort allowed her to slip out from the passenger seat and walk with Luke to their allotted unit.

Inside it was luxurious and not in the least utilitarian, and there was a splendid view of the city's lights from wide glassed windows. A terrace led off from the lounge, but Sally was conscious only of the adjoining bedroom, the closed front door, and the inescapable fact that they were now completely alone.

She was acutely aware of Luke surveying her with a deep unfathomable expression, and the silence seemed to grow until it became a huge threatening void, so that words—any words, were preferable.

'Would you like me to unpack?' Her voice sounded strange and stilted.

'Eager to assume your wifely duties?' Luke parried, and Sally felt a faint stirring of anger.

'I don't imagine you'll allow me to be neglectful of any of them.'

Luke's eyes narrowed slightly, and his lips moved in

a mere facsimile of a smile. 'Particularly in the bed-room?'

'There least of all,' she flung incautiously, taking a backward step as he moved close. It took all her cour-age to remain where she was. 'I'm not a willing part-ner—you must know that,' she ventured defiantly, hugging her arms together across her breasts as if that action would somehow protect her.

'You are either incredibly naive or deliberately play-ing the innocent. Which, I wonder?' he drawled mus-ingly.

'The latter, of course!' Sally exclaimed with in-tended sarcasm, uncaring that she implied otherwise.

He reached out a hand and idly tilted her chin. 'Ah, yes. Dewy-eyed virgins have become a rarity beyond the age of eighteen in our so-called enlightened society. Emancipation of women, and the freedom of equality, hmm?'

She suddenly had great difficulty in swallowing, for there seemed to be a lump in her throat that wouldn't subside. 'I'll go and unpack,' she managed quietly, and escaped his hold.

In the bedroom she took as much time as she dared to hang clothes into the wardrobe, placing remaining articles into the drawer space available. Then with a sense of icy fatalism she gathered up a nightgown and robe together with assorted toiletries, and made for the bathroom.

By the time she emerged she was consumed with a mixture of sheer nerves and a cold unshakable sense of rage that she had allowed herself to be coerced into such an alliance.

Only the lamp beside the bed was alight, and she almost stopped still at the sight of Luke in the process of discarding his clothes. With total unconcern for her presence he divested the last remaining garment and slid on a towelling robe before crossing to the bed.

A brilliant flood of colour warmed Sally's cheeks, and in a state of acute embarrassment she turned away on the pretext of hanging up the clothes she held over one arm.

'I do believe you are shy,' Luke drawled, and she started visibly at the sound of his voice so close behind her. His fingers released the ribbon that held her hair, so that it cascaded down to her shoulders, and she felt his fingers thread lightly through its silky length. 'Do not play the child, Sally,' he warned softly, tugging her hair, and she retorted swiftly,

'I'm not *playing* at anything.' A shiver of fear slid down her spine as he turned her round to face him, and she lifted a hand to smooth back a stray tendril of hair in a gesture that was purely mechanical.

'You would escape if you could, and flee into the night.' His voice was sardonic and full of amused cynicism, as with slow deliberate movements he slid the robe from her shoulders and let it fall to the floor, then his hands curved over the delicate bones of her shoulders, drawing her close.

Fear was replaced by anger the instant his head began to descend, and she turned her face aside, struggling with all her strength to fight free of his embrace. Not that it did the slightest good, for Luke thwarted each attempt with remarkable ease, and his soft laugh close to her ear was the last straw.

'Oh!' she gasped furiously, hating him with every nerve in her body. 'You're a barbaric—*savage*!' she accused, sorely tried, as his mouth continued its exploratory path, touching the delicate hollows beneath her throat, the pulsing cord at the side of her neck before travelling up to nuzzle an earlobe.

'Let go of me,' she implored, desperately trying to free her hands from behind her back where he held them together. Her shoulders and upper arms were beginning to ache with muscular strain, and her bosom heaved.

'Why fight me, *piccina*? You will become tired before we begin.'

'What did you expect?' she tossed bitterly as she drew a deep breath. 'A docile, amenable *lamb*?'

'If I had desired such a mate, I could have chosen one from any number of women,' Luke assured her musingly as he calmly lifted her into his arms and carried her towards the bed.

'I shall hate you,' Sally threatened furiously, only to hear his tigerish chuckle in response. Her back touched against the springy softness of the mattress, and she began struggling with every ounce of energy she possessed the moment his weight trapped her body.

Nothing moved him. Not even her pleas, or beseeching entreaty, and her only moment of satisfaction came when she managed to free her mouth from his for a brief second, long enough to sink her teeth into his shoulder.

His muttered curse was a sweet revenge, but only momentary, for he retaliated in kind on a much softer, more vulnerable part of her anatomy.

Sally gave a shocked whimper of pain and outrage, and pushed her hands against his chest in an effort to effect some sort of leverage. As her fingers came into contact with a liberal quantity of springy hair, she clenched and pulled—hard!

'Little she-cat,' he accused grimly. 'You are no chaste maiden—you admitted as much.' His voice was harsh and totally forbidding, and her desperate cry of protest died in her throat as his mouth fastened mercilessly on hers.

Oh dear God! The folly of her hastily-flung denial was bitter gall, and her sense of outrage increased as he sought with relentless persuasion to evoke an unwilling response, until, exhausted, she became caught up in the heaven and hell of his possession.

Later she lay at his side, cradled against him by an encircling arm, which even in sleep refused to allow her freedom. The slightest movement and his arm tightened about her, and at last she drifted into a storm-tossed sleep in which numerous demons chased and taunted her subconscious mind until the torment forced her into wakefulness in the early dawn hours.

Her whole body seemed one large ache, and she longed for a shower. Cautiously she moved an inch or two towards the side of the bed, then gradually eased her way free of Luke's sleep-heavy arm. Mercifully he seemed unaware, and she managed to slip to her feet.

The contact of soap and water on her skin provoked tingling sensations of an almost sensual quality, and with something akin to anger she scrubbed beneath the shower until her skin was aglow and rosy-pink from top to toe. Only then did she complete her toilette and slip silently back into bed.

There was a subtle aroma of freshly-brewed coffee wafting on the air, and combined with the tantalising smell of grilled bacon and toast, it teased Sally into wakefulness.

At first she was unsure of her surroundings, then returning memory brought reality sharply into focus, and she slowly turned and raised her head. Of Luke there was no sign, and a glance at her wristwatch revealed that it was late—a few minutes past ten, to be exact. Remarkably she had slept, despite a firm conviction that such blissful release would be an impossibility.

Quietly slipping from the bed, she collected fresh underwear, a skirt and top, then hurriedly slipped out of her nightgown. The day stretched mercifully ahead of her—until darkness fell and she had to face whatever the night would bring. A wry grimace passed fleetingly across her features. How women could rhapsodise over such indignities was beyond her!

Scorning any use of make-up, she ran a comb through her hair and decided her appearance would pass muster. Then she lifted her chin, took a deep breath, and determinedly made her way towards the kitchen.

Luke's broad frame was instantly visible, and a brief glance was all Sally needed to set her pulse-beat accelerating at an alarming rate. Sheer nerves, she dismissed crossly. Attired in grey suede trousers and a casual navy shirt, he projected a physical magnetism that was impossible to ignore.

'*Buon giorno.*'

He must have heard her enter the room, and after a momentary pause Sally made a slightly strangled rejoinder.

'Shall I pour the coffee?' She had to make some attempt at normality.

'Please. I feel in need of it.'

It was impossible to gauge much from his voice, she decided warily as she moved towards the table. Out of the corner of her eye she saw him switch off the element and transfer the contents of the frying pan on to two plates.

'I'm not very hungry,' she ventured, eyeing the quantity of food on the plate he placed before her.

'Eat, Sally,' he commanded as he took the chair opposite.

At once her hackles began to rise. 'Surely you'll allow me the right to choose the quantity of food I eat?'

His gaze was disconcertingly level. 'If you must argue, at least wait until I have had breakfast.'

'Why?' she queried sweetly. 'Don't you function very well on an empty stomach?'

Dark eyes, alive and faintly cynical, swept slowly over her features, bringing a faint flush of colour to her cheeks. 'You are way out of your depth, Sally,' he drawled.

'After last night, one couldn't doubt it!'

'Did you expect a chaste kiss, and nothing more?'

Sally met his gaze with difficulty. 'You had no need to be so disgustingly—animalistic.'

One eyebrow rose in mocking query. 'You professed to have had experience,' he accorded dryly, 'and fought like a little hellcat. Had I known you were an innocent, I would have ensured that the initiation was less—uninhibited.'

'Forgive me if I don't believe you!'

'It could have been worse,' Luke declared cryptically, and she suppressed an involuntary shiver.

'I'll take my coffee out on to the terrace.' She needed to get away from this hateful, cynical man—even if it was only for ten minutes.

'I advise you to eat something. To travel on an empty stomach could prove uncomfortable.'

Her eyes met his reluctantly. 'We're not staying here?'

'What did you imagine I had in mind, *mia sposa*? Four days spent behind closed doors, and a continuous bedroom romp?' His lips twisted into a taunting smile.

'I see from your blushes that that is precisely what you thought. Do not tempt the devil in me, *cara*,' he warned implacably. 'Already more than once you have tried my patience, and found the consequences unpleasant. Go and drink your coffee,' he bade brusquely. 'You will find the daily newspaper on the table—no doubt the printed word is preferable to my company.'

Sally picked up her cup and saucer and made her escape through the open sliding door on to the terrace without so much as a backward glance.

The warmth of the sun caressed her face, and the air smelt fresh and clean as she slid out a chair from beneath the wrought-iron table. Unfolding the newspaper, she scanned the headlines, trying to concentrate on the contents as she sipped her coffee, but they escaped her interest and she turned over the pages without reading more than an item or two.

Her gaze kept straying out over the terrace towards the city and habour. People walking, driving cars, shopping. They seemed so small and insignificant from this distance, and she couldn't help wondering if their emotions were any less complicated than her own.

Half an hour later their suitcases were packed and standing neatly side by side by the door, and Sally looked up as Luke entered the bedroom.

'Ready?'

She nodded silently at his drawling query, and watched as he collected a suitcase in each hand.

'I will deposit these in the boot, then return the key to the office. Wait for me in the car.'

'What if I'm tempted to drive away without you?' The flippant words were out before she could stop them, and she almost flinched beneath his quelling stare.

'My, my, you are a perverse little baggage this morning.' His voice was infinitely dangerous, and she wondered what on earth was driving her along such a certain path to self-destruction. It was almost as if some inner gremlin had conquered her very reason.

'Where would I escape to?' she reasoned with disparaging bleakness. 'I'm in a strange country, and you have the airline tickets.' She laughed a trifle bitterly. 'I could seek help from the police. What a story—I can see the headlines ... "Runaway bride seeks refuge—husband in pursuit". And you would pursue, wouldn't you, Luke? After all, I'm a tangible form of collateral ensuring my father's indebtedness. Poor Daddy—if only he knew!'

'Get in the car, Sally, before I do something regrettable.' There was a formidable threatening quality in his tone that boded ill for anyone foolish enough to ignore it.

Without a word she preceded him from the unit and slipped into the passenger seat of the car. There was no feeling of victory at having aroused his temper—in fact, she questioned her sanity in doing so.

For more than two hours Sally sat in complete silence, unwilling to venture anything by way of conversation to ease the journey to wherever it was that Luke had decided upon as their destination. Once, a spontaneous laugh bubbled to her lips as the actions of a young calf with its mother provided a humorous spectacle too difficult to ignore, and momentarily forgetting her quarrel she had glanced across to direct his attention, but one look at those stern saturnine features was sufficient to still even a glimmer of amusement.

The countryside was attractive, with gently rolling hillsides and green pasture, neat fences penning an alternate variety of cattle and sheep.

A gnawing hunger began in the pit of her stomach,

a vivid reminder of her stubborn refusal to eat breakfast. She wanted to ask where they were going, when
they could expect to arrive, and how long they would
stay. And especially, when they would eat!

'You are hungry?'

'If I say yes, will you refrain from saying, "I told
you so"?' Sally parried.

'We are almost there,' Luke answered blandly, and
she couldn't resist querying,

'Where is "there"?'

A slight smile twisted his lips. 'Rotorua—a tourist
resort famed both for its Maori culture and for being
one of the few places in the world where the earth's
surface is thinnest. Hence the wealth of mineral pools,
geysers, and pools of boiling mud. Can you not smell
the sulphur fumes?'

Sally wrinkled her nose. 'Is that what it is?' She
couldn't decide whether it was pleasant or otherwise.
No doubt one became accustomed to it!

Within a very short time they were negotiating the
main street, and she looked about her with interest.
There were several people walking—tourists, she pre-
sumed, from the number with cameras slung around
their necks.

'The motel is situated opposite the Gardens,' Luke
informed her, sparing her a glance. 'We will check in,
then find a place to eat.'

Their unit was one of several built around an inner
courtyard, in which a large swimming pool figured
prominently with crystal clear water that sparkled beneath the sun, and Sally cast it an envious glance, determined to spend some time in its beckoning coolness
before the day was over.

A quick application of lipstick, a comb run casually
through her hair, and she was ready to go to lunch.

In the restaurant adjoining the motel Luke ordered wine, which Sally declined, preferring to begin with undisguised appetite the delectable ham salad that was placed before her. With fresh fruit to follow, it proved a most enjoyable meal.

'Shall we embark on a tour through Whakare-warewa?'

Sally looked at her husband over the rim of her coffee cup, then placed it back on to the saucer and gave a negligent shrug. 'Whatever you say.'

Luke's eyes narrowed fractionally. 'We will drive around the Lakes tomorrow, and visit one or two of the trout springs. Then I had in mind to drive through to Lake Taupo, and head north on Monday. The Bay of Islands is particularly picturesque, and we will make a point of arriving in Auckland by mid-morning—I am sure you will display a feminine interest in a tour of the city's shops?'

Indeed, she echoed silently. 'I shall inveigle you into spending lavishly on anything that takes my fancy,' she answered lightly.

'Perhaps I had better purchase another suitcase?'

'That would be a good idea,' Sally endorsed sweetly, and glimpsed his mocking smile.

For the remainder of the afternoon they strolled along the designated paths through the scenic park with its steaming pools, geysers, and pools of boiling mud that were a source of amazement. There were petrified trees, a greyish-white, that stood stark and slightly ghoulish against the skyline. A Maori guide relayed folklore, explaining the significance of the meeting houses with their intricate carvings. One cool freshwater pool held a particular fascination, for there were several young Maori boys poised and ready to dive for any silver coins the tourists chose to throw into the clear water below, and their cheerful bartering brought smiles and goodnatured laughter from many an onlooker.

'If you've no objection, I'll go for a swim,' Sally decided almost as soon as they entered the motel unit shortly after five o'clock. The climate was slightly cooler than Sydney, but it was quite hot, nonetheless.

'Why should I object?' Luke questioned, lifting a faintly cynical eyebrow as she removed a bikini from her suitcase. 'I may even join you.'

'You could always stand on the sideline,' she couldn't resist taunting as she held the two scanty pieces of material aloft.

'An effective watchdog?'

'Somehow I can't imagine you indulging in an aimless frolic in the pool,' she retorted dryly, and caught his soft laugh.

'No? At thirty-seven, I hardly have one foot in the grave,' he returned mockingly, and she grimaced.

'You were never *young*, Luciano Andretti. I'm sure you came into this world having lived to the fullest extent in another. It shows in your eyes. There's nothing you haven't experienced, is there?' she ended a trifle bitterly.

'I am a self-made man, *cara*,' he declared sardonically, leaning with negligent ease against the door-frame. 'My parents died within months of each other when I was but a mere youth. My sister was brought up by the good Catholic Sisters—*I* worked day and night for anyone who would employ me. In the bowels of the earth, on cargo ships, in construction gangs—in almost every country in Western Europe. When I was not working, I studied—mathematics, languages. Fifteen years ago Angelina and I emigrated to Australia. Hard work and a series of shrewd investments have made me a reasonably wealthy man,' he concluded with a measure of cynicism.

'And your sister?' Sally couldn't help querying curiously. 'What became of her?'

'She is happily married with three children—aged respectively, four, two, and six months. I am a devoted uncle,' he informed her mockingly, 'and a frequent visitor to their home in Surfers' Paradise. We will spend Christmas there.'

She digested this piece of information, then ventured slowly, 'Does your sister know about me?'

'Angelina knows I have acquired a wife—yes.'

'But not why?'

'She will be content that someone has at last persuaded me to lead a life of respectability,' he said dryly, and a wry smile twisted his lips. 'Without doubt, she will begin counting the months until we make her an aunt.'

Sally felt the tide of tell-tale colour tinge her cheeks, and she abruptly turned away, saying in a slightly strangled voice, 'I'm going for a swim.'

'I will join you in a few minutes,' Luke intimated smoothly, his smile broadening as she collected a towel and fled rapidly from the room.

The water was deliciously cool, and Sally emerged to the surface from a plunging dive to smooth her hair and allow the excess water to run off her face. Apart from a few spectators enjoying a pre-dinner drink, the pool and its surrounding paved area was almost deserted.

A dark figure broke the water, and she turned to see Luke close by. An imp within prompted her to dive swiftly and head for the other end, and for a few brief seconds she thought her efforts to elude him were successful. However, a grip on her ankle followed simultaneously by a hard downward tug proved otherwise, and the next second she was pulled beneath the surface to be held there by an iron-like grip at her waist. The weight of the water made a mockery of any attempt to break free, and she gave an indignant gasp as they broke the surface together.

'Oh! Of all the——'

'A frolic, I think you said?' Luke teased, his eyes alight with devilish laughter, and at once she sought to retaliate.

Each attempt proved in vain, and sorely tried she scooped a handful of water and sent it cascading into his face. A tigerish growl escaped his lips an instant before his mouth settled on hers, and she threshed angrily, hating him afresh. An extra eight inches in height allowed him to stand on the pool's floor, whereas her legs could only flail in space.

The kiss was a teasing punishment, and deliberately evocative. When he lifted his head, her face was flushed and her eyes were bright with anger.

'There are people watching!' Sally hissed resentfully, and Luke merely laughed. 'Don't you care?' she queried, scandalised.

'Ah, *piccina*,' he mocked gently, 'what is so terrible about a husband kissing his wife?'

'We're causing a public spectacle,' she whispered fiercely. 'Let me go!'

'Too timid to share the joke, and kiss me back?' he baited softly, and she suddenly couldn't meet his gaze. With a subdued chuckle he allowed her to escape, and she swam to the side with swift strokes, lifting her body on to the ledge with a single elegant thrust.

By the time she reached their unit, Luke was only a

step behind, and once inside she viewed him warily. He was an unknown quantity and therefore unpredictable.

'Shall I use the shower first?' she faltered hesitantly, glimpsing the studied mockery evident in his expression.

'No doubt it would offend your sense of modesty if I suggest we take one together,' he drawled with intended wickedness, and Sally bit back a choking retort.

He was the most impossible, *devilish* man she had ever encountered, she determined crossly as she stepped beneath the warm needlespray minutes later. No doubt he thought her lack of sophistication and *savoir faire* amusing. The mocking *'piccina'* merely endorsed it! How she'd like to shock that look of worldly cynicism from his hateful face!

Sheer bravado made her select the most sophisticated evening gown in her wardrobe, and she spent considerable time and effort with her make-up, although her hair was confined into a knot wound on top of her head. She hadn't thought to bring her blowdryer, and the length of her hair precluded quick drying.

'My, my,' Luke drawled appreciatively, deliberately allowing his eyes to rove slowly over her figure. 'From your glamorous attire, I take it you want to dine in style?'

Sally forced herself to meet his gaze. 'Why not?' she countered lightly. 'I mean to make the most of my brief vacation from kitchen duties.'

'I did not marry you merely to gain a cook,' he rebuked.

'We *know* why you married me,' she declared dryly.

'The only light on the horizon is the fact that it won't be for ever.'

The sudden silence seemed almost a tangible entity. Sally could hear the thud of her heartbeats, and there was a painful tightness in her chest, restricting her breathing.

'I distinctly recollect stating that the arrangement was permanent,' Luke declared softly. 'If I had wanted a transitory alliance, I would not have insisted on something as legally binding as marriage.'

'It will never work,' she cried desperately.

'So sure—so soon?'

'I dislike you intensely,' she vociferated. 'How can we share a peaceful existence?'

'Come, *mia sposa*,' he bade sardonically, taking hold of her arm. 'We shall dine together at one of the better restaurants, and allow the tomorrows to take care of themselves, hmm?'

'Would you like to dance?'

Sally spared Luke a hesitant glance over the rim of her cup. They had enjoyed an excellent meal, consumed a bottle of wine, and were now lingering over coffee. It was late, well after eleven, and she felt inexplicably weary. Nothing would have pleased her more than to suggest they retire to their motel unit.

'Yes,' she agreed, and contrived the semblance of a smile as he guided her on to the dance floor. The music was soft and slow, necessitating conventional close contact.

'An attempt to delay the inevitable?' Luke queried mockingly. 'You look all eyes, and more than ready for bed.'

Sally stiffened in his arms, then tilted her chin so that she met his faintly cynical expression. 'I doubt I'll be permitted to sleep,' she snapped resentfully. 'Must I pay compound interest on my father's debt *every* night?'

There was a formidable silence—one that seemed to stretch for countless seconds, until she felt close to screaming with nervous tension. Dear Lord in heaven, what was the matter with her? He was able to provoke her into saying the most insulting things. A shimmer of self-pitying tears momentarily clouded her vision, and she looked away, blinking rapidly.

In something of a daze, she found herself being led back to their table where Luke caught up her gossamer wrap and after settling the bill, he ushered her out into the cool evening air. The car was driven the short distance to their motel with a swift competence that disguised the tightly leashed anger Sally sensed beneath the surface of his control.

Once inside their unit, she preceded him into the lounge and turned to regard him warily. His eyes were dark and deliberately enigmatic, making it impossible to judge his mood.

'I'm not afraid of you,' Sally proclaimed bravely. Liar! Why else was she trembling?

'You should be,' Luke retorted grimly. 'For a moment, you came dangerously close to feeling the lash of my temper.' He moved across the room with catlike fluidity to pause a few inches in front of her, then reaching out, he caught hold of her shoulders.

Sally felt a shiver slip down the length of her spine as his mouth fastened on hers, forcing open her lips in a kiss that was deliberately punishing in its intent. Just as she thought it might go on for ever, his mood changed, and his touch assumed a sensual quality as his lips sought the sensitive pulse at the base of her throat and trailed down the deep vee of her gown to the exposed cleft between her breasts. Any attempt to break free from his embrace proved fruitless, and there was a strange warmth invading her lower limbs as his mouth travelled up to claim her lips. This time there was none of the relentless pressure as, warm and disruptively probing, he evoked a response she was unable to prevent.

A strange weightlessness seemed to prevail, and she was faintly aware that they had somehow progressed from the lounge to the bedroom. The release of the long zipper on her evening gown brought a returning sanity and an instinctive desire to struggle out of his arms. Hands pushed against his chest as her panic rose, and she twisted her face away in an effort to break free of those warm, seducing lips.

Luke allowed her to step back a pace as his hands slid down to her waist, imprisoning her so that she couldn't escape completely, and there was a glint of humour evident in the lazy glance he slanted down at her.

'There is not an inch of your body my lips have not explored,' he drawled, deliberately catching hold of her hands as he eased the gown over her shoulders and let it fall to the carpet. 'It is a little too late to display reticence.'

'You're hateful!' she cried angrily as he slipped the clip on her bra and tossed it aside.

'You married a man, *mia sposa*,' he taunted softly, 'not an ineffectual mouse who would beg for his wife's favours.'

'An insensitive, uncaring—*brute*!' Sally accused, struggling fiercely to free her hands from behind her back. Not that it did much good, for her puny strength was no match against his.

'Who takes what he wants, hmm? And I do want

you, *piccina*. To taste the honey-sweetness of you, and to feel you quivering in my arms.'

'I don't want *you*!' she assured vehemently, becoming breathless from exertion. 'That knowledge should be bittersweet.'

'Ah, Sally,' he mocked, 'only moments ago you responded involuntarily. Admit it, if you dare.'

'You're a loathsome, arrogant—devil!' she thrust angrily. 'I have bruises everywhere from last night, and I ache all over.'

With slow deliberate movements he unbuttoned his shirt and shrugged it off his shoulders, transferring his grip on her hands as he tossed the shirt to the floor.

'I was very careful not to bruise you,' he said quietly. With his free hand he indicated a circle of teeth marks on one sinewy shoulder. 'Except in direct retaliation to this.'

Sally's eyes widened measurably, and she felt utterly shocked as she saw the large darkening bruise surrounding several sharply-defined marks.

'Your fingernails are sharp, like miniature daggers,' Luke continued in a significant drawl, his eyes openly sardonic. 'You also beat a mean fist. If a count of battle-scars were taken, *piccina*, mine would undoubtedly outnumber yours.'

'You hurt me,' she cried, unwillingly provoked, and saw his wry smile.

'Since you had never known a man, a certain—wounding was inevitable. I can promise that tonight will be different.'

Sally swallowed convulsively, and tried to ignore the way her stomach curled at his words. 'I'd rather be left alone. I—I have a headache,' she invented wildly.

'That is both unoriginal and untrue,' he answered softly, pulling her irresistibly forward until she was moulded against the hard length of him. His lips sought hers, incredibly gentle as with undoubted mastery he began urging alive the hidden fire deep within.

A tiny moan of entreaty escaped as she resisted the desire to melt beneath his touch, and she fought desperately against the aching need for fulfilment as his caresses aroused sensations she hadn't known existed. It was like drowning slowly in a blissful pool of warmth, making her utterly mindless and incapable of coherent thought.

It wasn't until later as she lay in his sleeping arms that the resentment began to flare. She hated him— but even more, she hated her traitorous body for responding with a will all of its own.

CHAPTER FIVE

THEIR remaining three days on New Zealand soil were expended touring steadily northward, taking in the Bay of Islands and Russell, the city of Whangarei, followed by a leisurely drive down to Auckland on Monday evening.

The days Sally enjoyed—the nights, however, were something else. No matter how stiff an exterior she presented, Luke was able to dispense with any resistance, and the knowledge irked her unreasonably.

Tuesday morning Luke kept his word by indulging her in a shopping spree, and after frequenting two of the downtown duty-free shops for souvenirs, they explored several arcades before entering a large department store.

'That is very chic,' Luke observed, indicating a mannequin adorned in a red gown of filmy organza with an elegant handkerchief skirt. The bodice was quite plain, fitting firmly over the bosom, with a single shoestring strap crossing over each shoulder. 'You must try it on.'

Sally turned and smiled. 'Are you serious? It may not be my size.'

He took her arm and led her towards a hovering saleswoman, directing with considerable charm that the gown be removed. Not content, he murmured that he wished something in blue be brought for their approval. And when Sally caught sight of a blouson-styled shirtwaister dress in soft floral chiffon, he indicated that as well.

'Luke,' she couldn't help protesting, 'I have plenty

of clothes. Besides, there's not room for anything else in my suitcase.'

'Then we shall buy another,' he responded tolerantly. 'Go into the changing room, Sally, and you will come out and let me see each dress as you try it on.'

The temptation to give a short curtsy was too much to resist, and she caught the amusement in those dark eyes as she turned and disappeared from sight.

They all fitted her perfectly, but if she had to select one, it would be the red gown. The colour seemed to highlight her hair and add a glow to her skin.

'We will take all three,' Luke instructed, and Sally hid a smile at the saleswoman's obvious delight, and for her benefit Sally stood dutifully on tiptoe and brushed his cheek with her lips.

'Thank you, darling.'

Afterwards they had lunch in the bistro bar of a nearby hotel, then drove to the motel in Parnell where they deposited their parcels before emerging to walk the short distance to Parnell Village.

The converted old houses were picturesque, remodelled into shops and boutiques, and Sally fell in love with the atmosphere the Village projected. Cobblestone bricks with moss between the cracks and spaces formed walkways between the shops, and there were several that sported multi-paned bay windows in which the wares were displayed.

'Oh, how beautiful!' Sally couldn't help the soft exclamation as she saw a delicate cobwebby handcrafted shawl in the tiny bay window of a shop down a narrow lane. The hours that must have gone into its making were surely numerous, and she had a mental picture of a tiny white-haired old lady sitting in a rocking-chair with her head bent over wool and crochet hook as she worked.

'Ah, yes,' Luke murmured close beside her. 'It is exquisite, is it not? It will go well with the red gown.'

'You intend buying it?' she queried incredulously, and he smiled.

'You object?'

'No—it's just that I didn't admire it with the intention of——'

'Shall we go into the shop?' he suggested musingly. 'This lane is very narrow, and there are others wishing to pass.'

For a further hour they wandered in and out of the many shops in the Village, and Sally added a few purchases of her own—mementoes, and a gift for her father. Then it was time to go back to the motel to complete their packing, for they had to leave for the airport at four-thirty.

The early evening flight deposited them in Sydney shortly before eight o'clock, and after an uncomplicated inspection by Customs, they emerged into the reception lounge to be greeted by Carlo, and—surprise—Joe Ballinger, both smiling expansively.

'Daddy!' Sally flew into her father's outstretched arms with an enthusiasm that caused him to pat her shoulder with slight concern.

'Heavens, child,' he chided laughingly, 'anyone would think you'd been gone for four months, instead of four days!'

She drew back self-consciously, then managed an over-bright smile. 'You're all the family I have.'

'Am I forgotten so quickly?' Luke mocked gently, and she shook her head.

'You're not in the same category as my father.'

'I should hope not, *cara*.'

At the sound of her husband's drawling response, she turned and projected him a sweet smile. 'Darling

Luke, you're one of a kind.'

Luke inclined his head slightly in acknowledgment, although his eyes were peculiarly lacking in humour.

Carlo took charge of the suitcases, implying that he would stow them in the boot, then bring the car round to the main entrance.

'You'll come back with us for a drink, won't you?' Sally appealed to her father, uncaring whether Luke would approve the invitation. Anything to delay being alone with him in that huge mansion in Vaucluse—for, once there, she would be made indisputably aware that she was little more than an acquisition with a particular purpose in mind. Hostess, cook-cum-housekeeper on occasion, but foremost was that of human breeding-machine! Children she liked, and she found babies adorable. Any prior thought she might have given to her own had always evolved from a loving relationship, and far removed from the cold, calculating manner Luke had chosen.

'Sally—no,' Joe refused without any regret, adding gently, 'It's your first night home. In a few days, perhaps.' He smiled at her obvious disappointment. 'I'm giving a dinner party at the end of next week. You'll both come, of course?'

'Thank you, Joe,' Luke answered smoothly, and taking Sally by the arm he began leading the way through the mingling crowd. 'We will let you know. I may be out of town.'

Sally cast him a startled glance, and caught his faint smile.

'I have a business to run, *cara*—remember?'

Joe gave a hearty laugh, and winked at his daughter. 'The honeymoon is over!'

How I wish it had never begun, Sally declared silently.

The Alfa-Romeo with Carlo at the wheel was visible through the glass doors, and in a matter of minutes Luke handed her into the rear seat, then slid in beside her. Joe became an increasingly distant waving figure as Carlo set the car in motion.

In less than half an hour they would be home—Luke's home, never hers, Sally mused broodingly. Why, she hadn't seen any of it, except the kitchen, dining-room and lounge. Quite what the ground floor comprised she could only surmise, although it seemed logical to conclude that the bedrooms were situated on the third and upper floor. The thought of being able to explore gave her a sense of pleasure.

'Tired?'

Sally cast the man at her side a slightly startled look. 'Not really. I was thinking.'

'Pleasant thoughts, I hope?'

Conscious of Carlo within hearing distance, she tempered her reply with seeming affection. 'It will be nice to get home and unpack everything.' She even managed a light laugh. 'I hope you've plenty of spare wardrobe space, darling.'

For an answer Luke caught one of her hands and lifted it to his lips, holding it effortlessly while he kissed each fingertip in turn, and his eyes remained fixed on hers, openly sardonic, daring her to utter anything by way of remonstrance. It was a relief when the car swept up into the Vaucluse end of New South Head Road, slowing to a halt in the wide sweeping driveway a few minutes later.

Carlo preceded them, carrying the luggage, and once inside Luke paused, sweeping an arm to the right.

'Aside from a few service rooms, there is only garage space on this level. To the left are Carlo's living quarters.' He led the way towards the wide staircase leading up to the first floor. 'Both the lounge and the formal dining-room you have already seen, but opposite and adjacent to the kitchen is a smaller dining-room, as well as another lounge, or *salotto*, where you will find a television set, stereo, several bookcases filled with books. And in seclusion on this side of the stairs is my study.'

The uppermost floor was an area hitherto unseen, and Sally expressed surprise over the number of bed-rooms—five in all, the largest being the master bed-room with en suite facilities, as well as two separate bathrooms further down the hall.

However, it was the main bedroom that held her attention. The colours blended delightfully, from the deep cream and beige shaggy carpet to the wild-rice coloured floor-to-ceiling drapes, the dark satin-mahogany furniture that was essentially continental in design, and the dark chocolate-brown velvet bed-spread. The walls were sculpture-plastered in cream, and the swirling design was effective.

'I am sure you will find plenty of space for your clothes,' Luke drawled a trifle dryly. 'If you discover the necessity to rearrange any of my clothing, please tell me—I do not relish playing "hunt the thimble" for my underwear.'

'If I do, I'll draw you a diagram,' Sally responded hollowly, her thoughts running riot over the number of women who might have shared that opulent bed.

'The answer is none,' he assured her blandly, and she gave him a look of disbelief. 'At least, not in *that* bed,' he elaborated with a decidedly wicked smile.

'Do you read minds?' she queried icily—an effect totally destroyed by the brilliant colour burning her cheeks.

'Yours is particularly transparent, *piccina*,' he

illuminated quizzically, and leaning out a hand he touched the warmth, then trailed his fingers down to begin a subtle disturbing caress along the sensitive cord of her neck. 'I have to acquaint myself with developments over the past few days—via a sheaf of data despatched from my office, and a tape. Carlo will make some coffee if you should want it, and I will have mine in the study. Do you mind?'

Sally met his gaze unblinkingly. 'Would it matter if I did?'

His smile broadened and became faintly mocking. 'I could be persuaded to leave it until morning. An hour before breakfast would be ample.'

'Far be it for me to keep you from your work. Besides,' she determined firmly, 'I want to unpack. I may even watch television for a while.'

A tigerish chuckle left his throat, then he leant down and bestowed a swift hard kiss on her unsuspecting lips before turning and leaving the room.

Alone, Sally followed her voiced intentions by unpacking, and after a leisurely shower she put on a robe and went downstairs to the *salotto*. There didn't seem to be anything outstanding on any of the television channels, so she crossed to the stereo equipment and selected three LP's. She was beginning to feel rather sleepy, but nothing could persuade her to go upstairs and slip between the covers of that large bed. Instead, she curled up on the settee with a cushion beneath her head, listening to the soothing strains of Rod Stewart's gravelly rendition of 'Sailing' float softly across the room. Her mind wandered a little as her father's image came to mind, and such thought brought a vivid reminder of her present predicament. If only she'd been born *ugly*...A tiny voice whispered tauntingly that if that were so, her father would now be facing bankruptcy, stripped of all his possessions, his pride dragging the dust. It was a chilling thought.

With something akin to resentment, she raised herself on one elbow and plumped the cushion with unnecessary force, then swept her hair aside and settled down again. Perhaps if she closed her eyes for a few minutes ...

When she awoke, it was daylight, and she was in bed —alone. A somewhat rumpled pillow and tossed covers on the opposite side indicated that Luke had lain beside her during the night. She didn't need to speculate that it was he who had carried her from the *salotto* and deposited her between the sheets. A glance at her wristwatch revealed that it was late—after nine, in fact. Hurriedly she swept the covers aside and gathered together some clothes.

She emerged into the kitchen some ten minutes later, feeling refreshed and longing for some coffee.

'*Buon giorno, signora.*' Carlo looked up from his task of frying eggs and gave Sally a polite smile.

'Good morning. I'm afraid I slept in.' She moved across the room to stand a few feet from the stove. 'Can I do anything to help?'

'*Grazie*—but no. Luke has already left for the city,' he informed her. 'He left instructions that you were not to be disturbed. As soon as I heard movements upstairs, I began cooking your breakfast.'

'You shouldn't have bothered,' Sally assured him kindly. 'I could easily have made it.' At the other's slightly scandalised expression, she had to suppress a smile. Quite obviously that had been the wrong thing to say!

Carlo dished eggs, bacon, and grilled tomatoes on to a plate, took toast from beneath the griller, and carried them to the table. Then he poured coffee, and indicated the neatly-folded daily newspaper. 'After the *signora* has eaten, may I suggest that any clothes for washing, or for the dry-cleaners, be put out? I will attend to them.'

Oh heavens, he surely wasn't going to keep on referring to her as 'the *signora*', was he? Aloud, she ventured tentatively, 'Couldn't you call me Sally?'

'If it pleases you.'

Sally subsided into a chair and sugared her coffee. It smelt delicious, and so did the contents of her plate. 'Have you worked for my husband for very long?' she queried idly.

'Five years as his employee, but I have known him many years.' He paused in thoughtful reflection. 'Some fourteen years ago we cut cane together in North Queensland, and a few years later we met again in Weipa where we worked for the same construction company. Six years ago I had to slow down a bit—the doctor said the heat, the dust, too much hard work is not good for my health. So I came south to Sydney. Luke and I met by chance, and'—he shrugged expansively, 'we talked, shared a few drinks. He offered me this position with him, and I took it. He is a good man,' he concluded with the utmost sincerity.

Sally was silent as she digested this information. 'Do you have anyone to help in the house?' she ventured at last.

'*Si*—twice a week a woman comes to help with the cleaning, and to do the ironing. Otherwise, I manage the rest.'

'Perhaps I could relieve you of some of the work—especially with regard to the meals.'

Carlo smiled. 'It is your kitchen, Sally,' he reminded her politely. 'Luke left the message that you will be dining out tonight, and requests you be ready to leave at seven—he expects to be home at approximately six o'clock.'

So she was to be thrust in at the deep end, socially, she perceived. Well, pleasant conversational patter was something in which she was well versed, thanks to her father. Although the thought of meeting Luke's friends, especially women friends, was slightly daunting.

Sally spent the rest of the morning exploring the spacious three-level mansion, and found pleasure in its design and furnishings. After a light lunch of salad and cheese, she telephoned her father only to find that he was out of the office. She'd wanted to speak to him, not for any specific reason other than to hear his voice, and to suggest he might like to meet her for lunch the following day.

Her collection of evening gowns was adequate, but one in particular was quite startling. Of creamy-white fine wool crêpe, it hugged her breasts, divided and curved round her neck, leaving the back bare to her waist. The skirt fell in soft folds to her ankles, and with it she wore a long silk-fringed stole wound round her neck with the ends flowing down her back. The complete outfit was demurely simple—an effect totally destroyed by removal of the stole.

The dinner proved to be a considerably larger affair than Sally had envisaged, with no fewer than twenty guests, and together they occupied two large tables in a secluded corner of one of Sydney's exclusive restaurants.

A tiny thrill of pleasure whispered down Sally's spine as she allowed her gaze to settle on her husband's superbly-tailored frame. He looked undeniably attractive—arresting, she amended silently. He was too rugged to be considered handsome, possessing a well-sculptured nose and the broad facial bone structure typical of his heritage. His mouth was wide, the lips sensuously moulded as they curved slightly at the corners. Added to which was the stamp of arrogance, an assurance wealth invariably provided, making the total effect one of dynamic masculinity.

Sally gleaned from their conversation that most of the men were business acquaintances. It was apparent that news of Luke's marriage had travelled swiftly, and she was aware of the speculation, the thinly-veiled curiosity from many of the women present. As the evening progressed she began to feel oddly vulnerable —rather like a lamb among the lions!

'You seem quiet,' Luke mused, leaning towards her. 'What is going on inside that head of yours?'

Sally gave him a wry smile. 'From the number of looks I've been receiving, you must have led a pretty intriguing sort of social existence!'

His expression assumed that of cynical amusement. 'All work and no play . . .' he drawled mockingly.

'Of course—a self-professed rake! The cause of so much conjecture can obviously be attributed to the fact that I don't possess the sophisticated panache associated with your usual—er—companions.'

'Eat your dessert, Sally,' he bade dryly, and Sally bestowed him a singularly beguiling smile.

'Why, *darling*—am I not sweet enough?'

'You, *amante*, are playing a very dangerous game,' he cautioned softly.

'And I should desist?' she queried with seeming innocence.

'Really, Luke!' a voice chided in mild reproof. 'Are old friends to be denied your attention?'

Sally glanced across the table and met the openly mocking gaze of a woman whose name for the moment escaped her. Unusual and faintly exotic—Carmela, that was it. Dark-haired, with olive skin, an hour-glass figure that bordered on voluptuousness, the woman had been making an obvious play for Luke's attention throughout the evening.

'Carmela, forgive me,' Luke drawled quizzically. 'I find my wife quite irresistible.' He leant out a hand and let it trail lightly down Sally's cheek. 'Dance with me, *cara*,' he commanded softly, and his eyes assumed a definite gleam as he glimpsed her barely concealed indignation. With seeming indolence he stood to his feet and caught hold of her hand.

Sally allowed herself to be led on to the dance floor, and as Luke gathered her into his arms she demanded furiously, 'Must you hold me so close?' Then she became utterly enraged when he bent low and kissed her mouth. It was a seal of possession, albeit brief, that rankled long after they had circled the floor.

'I think you're a perfect fiend!' she whispered fiercely when he showed no inclination to return to their table.

'This gown of yours is deceptive,' he observed musingly, and Sally wriggled a little as his hand moved in lazy exploration over her bare back. 'Are you wearing anything at all underneath it?'

'Of course,' she admitted, giving him a bewitching smile. 'My skin.'

Luke's subdued chuckle was her undoing, and she lifted her head to gaze angrily up at him.

'Steady, *cara*,' he warned softly. 'Whatever will my friends think if you display your childish temper?'

'I didn't know I possessed a temper until I met you!' she hissed furiously. 'As to your friends—most of those women would wish me dead!'

'Ah, *piccina*, could it be that you are jealous?'

'No,' she denied huskily, and she struggled in his arms only to find they had become steel bands holding her prisoner. 'I'd like to go home,' she pleaded evenly. 'I'm becoming tired of all the curious speculative glances——'

'My dear Sally, you are exaggerating,' he drawled, and she felt helplessly inadequate.

It was close on midnight when they did leave—and after almost two hours of smiling and participating in polite conversation Sally felt as if her face would crack! Once they were in the car, she sat close to the door, as far away from her hateful husband as the vehicle's interior would allow. Not once did she attempt to speak, and the entire twenty-minute journey was completed in silence.

Inside the house, she ran up the two flights of stairs with the intention of escaping, but it was a foolhardy exercise as Luke entered the bedroom brief seconds after, and his expression was anything but sympathetic.

'You are behaving like a spoilt child in need of a spanking,' he began hardly. 'A part of your education your father appears to have sadly neglected.'

'Oh, go to hell!'

For one terrible minute Sally thought he meant to strike her, and she flinched involuntarily from the cold anger emanating from his grim countenance. It was sure folly to clash with him, but she was goaded by heaven knew what. Some devil within wanted to rage and storm, driving her on against all sane reason.

'*Dio santo!*' Luke swore softly, pulling her resisting body close to his. One arm held her immobile from her shoulder down the length of her spine, while the other hand crept up to hold fast her head.

His mouth crushed hers, punishing until she thought

she couldn't stand it another minute, then at last he put her at arm's length. There were tears shimmering diamond-bright making her eyes appear huge pools of blue in a face that had become startlingly pale. Her lips felt bruised and swollen, and she could taste blood where he'd heartlessly ground the soft inner tissue against her teeth.

'I refuse to be judged by the vagaries of your vivid imagination,' he drawled ruthlessly.

'I—don't care if you've slept with a *hundred* different women,' Sally stammered painfully, running the tip of her tongue over lips that were trembling.

'You, sweet idiot, are more *child* than woman,' he murmured with wry exasperation.

'I wish I were!'

His smile was faint. 'So that you might sleep alone and dream sweet dreams? Ah, *cara*, would you have me believe you do not enjoy being a woman in my arms?' he mocked with deliberate cynicism.

Sally lifted her head erect, meeting his gaze. 'It proves precisely nothing—other than that you're accomplished in the art of seduction.'

Luke leant out an idle finger and touched the base of her throat. 'And this racing pulse-beat—what of it?'

Like a nervous filly, she jerked away from his scorching touch. 'Oh, why can't you leave me alone?' she implored. 'Haven't you punished me enough?'

His eyes narrowed fractionally, then he caught hold of her chin and held it firm. Gently he touched her lower lip, pulling it down despite her efforts to evade him. His barely audible oath confused her, for it was clearly self-derisory.

'That was unfair of me,' he offered quietly as he released her, and he trailed gentle fingers over the ravage he had caused. 'You have an incredibly soft mouth.'

His lips touched hers, moving slightly so that her own quivered and parted a little, then began a gentle exploration that was deliberately evocative, so that when he drew away she experienced a feeling of regret.

For a moment Luke surveyed her bemused expression, then he gave a soft laugh and swung her up into his arms to carry her with effortless ease towards the bed.

'You have no objection if we give an informal dinner for a few friends this evening?'

Sally looked across the breakfast table and met Luke's faintly quizzical glance. Her eyes widened with genuine surprise. 'No, of course not. How many do you have in mind?'

'Six, including ourselves. It is not too short notice?'

'I'm a professional cook, remember?' she reminded him lightly. 'Do you want anything in particular on the menu, or am I allowed carte blanche?'

'I am not your employer, Sally,' Luke chided wryly. 'Decide, and give Carlo a list of what you need. I will be home at six, and I shall direct our guests to arrive at seven.'

As soon as Luke departed for the city Sally began planning the food. Informal, he had decreed, but she instinctively felt she would be on trial as far as his guests were concerned, and therefore the dinner must be something special.

After much thought she decided on scallops *au gratin*, *filet mignon* as the main course, with *tulipe glacée* for dessert. She made out a list, checked the contents of the downstairs wine cellar, then despatched Carlo into the city for the items she required.

There was something infinitely appealing about preparing food for her own dinner party, as hitherto she had cooked for her father or in a professional capacity at 'Claude's', and the time seemed to slip by with an amazing speed. Carlo proved a willing ally, and she felt completely at ease accepting his help with the preparations. It was agreed that he would serve the meal so that she would be free to entertain the guests.

Sally decided to wear the red gown Luke had bought in Auckland, and as she slipped it on she couldn't help wondering who the four guests would be. Luke hadn't mentioned any names, and she was naturally curious. The mirror revealed a reflection that was definitely eye-catching, and she stood back well pleased with the effect. Her make-up complete, she toyed with the decision of putting her hair up, or leaving it loose. She wanted to look as sophisticated as possible—in a knot at her nape, perhaps, with a few tendrils escaping in wispy curls beside her ears, or a soignée french pleat?

'Leave it loose, *cara*—you look too much the school-marm with it pulled back.'

Sally turned slightly and caught Luke's amused expression as he crossed the room to her side. He had exchanged his business suit for suede trousers and a navy shirt, and he looked compellingly rugged. A tiny shiver iced its way down her spine as he bent and laid his lips against the back of her neck, and she experienced the most incredible desire to turn round and lift her face for his kiss. She didn't even like him, so why should she want his embrace? She had to be temporarily mad to entertain such a thought!

'Who is coming tonight?' she queried a trifle breathlessly, and missed his slight smile as she moved away on the pretext of selecting shoes.

'Peter Hampshire, who is a colleague of mine, and his wife Elaine,' Luke told her smoothly. 'Carmela

Ortega, and Rolf Unger. You've already met Carmela, I think?'

Oh yes—who could forget such an exotic beauty as Carmela? Inwardly her heart sank a little. There wasn't much point in attempting to appear sophisticated with Carmela present, for the other woman reduced her to schoolgirlish inadequacy at a glance!

'You look very beautiful, *piccina*,' Luke drawled, and she was stung into retorting rather peevishly,

'Why must you call me that? I feel nervous enough without being referred to as a child!'

'Ah, *cara*, it is only a teasing nickname, nothing more.' He chuckled huskily and leant out a hand to wind a strand of long blonde hair round his finger. 'I assure you I think of you as anything but infantile.' He gave a gentle tug, turning her round to face him, and she searched his expression for something behind the amused indulgence.

'I think I'll have a glass of sherry.' She gave a light laugh, and endeavoured to smile. 'I'm suffering from a mild case of nerves.'

'Then let us go down to the lounge,' Luke directed, taking hold of her elbow.

Afterwards, Sally was glad that she had chosen to wear the red gown, for Carmela's black gown was anything but the 'little basic black' one kept for any occasion, and it enhanced her generous curves to perfection.

'Carlo has excelled himself,' Carmela complimented as the main course was removed and dessert placed on the table. She lifted her glass and took a generous sip of wine. 'Only in a restaurant have I sampled *filet mignon* such as that.'

Luke directed Sally a warm smile. 'You must compliment my wife.'

At once Carmela's eyebrows arched in disbelief. 'Sally? Good heavens, my dear,' she murmured, 'you are indeed fortunate in acquiring a wife who can cook as well as look so incredibly'—she paused fractionally to smile at Sally—'young.'

Elaine Hampshire cast Sally a sympathetic glance, and Sally inwardly seethed as Luke gave a subdued chuckle of amusement.

'Darling,' she managed with deliberate emphasis, 'may I have some more wine?' She didn't really want her glass refilled, but she needed something to cool her temper! Carmela Ortega was a positive *cat*!

Shortly afterwards they retired to the lounge for coffee, and Sally couldn't help noticing that Carmela declined to stand with Elaine, preferring instead to join the three men.

'Do you have any children?' Sally queried of Elaine, and the other woman gave an amused smile.

'Two young teenagers, who alternately delight and despair. Keeping up with them takes most of my energy.'

'Have you and Peter known Luke very long?'

'Seven years,' Elaine told her. 'Peter works with Luke.'

Sally swallowed slightly, feeling momentarily embarrassed. 'I didn't know, I'm sorry.'

'My dear, there's no need to apologise. Rolf also is employed by your husband—Carmela, too, although more indirectly. '

'Oh, I see.'

The other smiled kindly. 'You haven't been married very long. I imagine informing you about his business associates hasn't been uppermost in Luke's mind.'

It was a successful evening overall, although Sally would have felt more at ease without Carmela's pres-

ence. It irked her considerably that Luke appeared not
to notice Carmela's deliberate attempts to gain his
attention, and by the time their guests left, she was a
quietly seething ball of fury.

'*Grazie, mia sposa*, for providing an excellent
dinner.'

Sally gave Luke a singularly sweet smile before
turning to precede him up the first flight of stairs. 'I
am pleased to be of some use,' she threw over her
shoulder, her voice heavy with emphasis.

Luke entered the bedroom and closed the door. 'My
dear Sally,' he drawled musingly, 'sarcasm does not become you.' He began walking towards her, and she
darted towards the bathroom with the intention of
evading him.

'Go, *piccina*,' he mocked gently. 'If you are not in
bed within ten minutes, I shall come and fetch you.'

'Oh, is that all you can think about?' she flung
angrily, and saw his eyes gleam with sardonic amusement.

'Would you rather I did not desire you, *cara*?' he
taunted softly, and she closed the bathroom door with
a decisive snap.

It was becoming difficult to win any battles against
him, and what was more, she wasn't sure she wanted
to.

The following day Sally met her father for lunch, after
first ringing him at work and inveigling the invitation.

She felt vaguely guilty as she slipped into the chair
held out for her by a hovering waiter, and the look she
directed across the table drew raised eyebrows.

'You look like a schoolgirl who's hidden the teacher's
chalk and about to be found out,' Joe Ballinger declared. 'Want to confess?'

Sally smiled, then made a wry grimace. 'I've spent rather a lot of my husband's money—a new evening gown, to be precise. And shoes,' she concluded.

'Luke appears to be an indulgent husband. Why should he mind?' Joe questioned mildly.

Because I didn't really need a new gown, she declared silently. It was one of those wild spur-of-the-moment spending sprees that she was now beginning to regret. The sane, logical part of her was appalled at having spent more than a month's salary on one gown. Aloud, she prevaricated, 'Luke presented me with some credit cards this morning. We're spending Christmas with his sister and her family, and he likes to play the benevolent uncle. I've been supplied with a list as long as my arm outlining what gifts to buy, and for whom.' She looked at her father and experienced a feeling of sadness. 'What will you do over Christmas, Daddy? It won't be the same without you.'

'Sally!' he chided laughingly. 'Your place is with your husband, not your father.' He leant across the table and took hold of her hand. 'I shall go to my Club for a few hours—they put on a very good Christmas dinner, so I'm told. There'll be other Christmases,' he added briskly. 'Now, tell me what you thought of New Zealand—or, in the style of true honeymooners, didn't you see very much of anything, except each other?'

Oh God, what could she say in answer to that? 'What do you think?' she queried, and even managed a light laugh.

'You *are* happy, aren't you, Sally?'

This was even worse than she imagined! 'There would be something wrong with me if I weren't,' she assured him evenly. 'What more could I ask for?'

'I must admit I was rather anxious when you sprang the marriage on me,' her father reflected. 'It was impossible not to be sceptical. Although, once I'd given it some thought, I could see why you were both attracted to each other. And after all, there was no reason to have a long engagement. Besides,' he paused humorously, 'Luke has a reputation for getting what he wants. I don't think you fully appreciate his business acumen, Sally. Your husband is a very clever, astute man.'

'I wrote to Mummy,' Sally ventured. 'You'd better be prepared to receive a trans-Atlantic call in about three days' time.' She gave him an impish grin. 'She'll want to reassure herself that her daughter hasn't done anything foolish. I gave her my telephone number as well—otherwise she might think it necessary to catch the next flight to Sydney!'

Joe burst into unrestrained laughter. 'Knowing Emily, she'll do just that, anyway!' He withdrew a handkerchief and wiped his eyes. 'Oh, my dear. One of us really should warn Luke about your darling mother!'

'What say we let her surprise him?' she suggested wryly. 'She may not come at all—especially if she's satisfied with the answers she receives over the telephone.'

'Most unlikely, don't you think?'

'Quite,' Sally agreed.

'Well, dear girl,' Joe said regretfully, glancing at his watch, 'I must get back to work. Two new contracts have fallen into our lap, and the estimates must be gone over with a fine toothcomb before I submit them for Luke's approval.'

'Luke?' she queried, sipping the last of her coffee.

Joe nodded. 'Didn't you know? He's bought into the company. I supervise the workmen and materials, and Luke handles the financial side. The profits are to be divided proportionately, and I receive a managerial salary.'

Sally digested this piece of information slowly. 'He doesn't discuss business with me,' she said at last. 'How do you feel about the arrangement?'

'It relieves me of any worry. The more I think about it, the more I realise how fortunate I am in having someone with Luke's financial wizardry behind me. Now, I really must go. Don't forget my dinner party next Friday evening.'

'Let me cook it for you,' she pleaded with sudden inspiration. 'It can be an early Christmas dinner—not necessarily Christmas fare, but I'd love to—really,' she assured him as he looked doubtful. 'Luke won't mind.' Well, I hope he won't, she reflected idly, but even if he does object, I'll do it anyway!

'That would be nice,' Joe agreed. 'Ring me when you've obtained his approval.'

Luke, however, was adamant in his refusal when she broached the subject.

'Why?' Sally queried coldly, feeling the familiar resentment begin to unfurl. 'What possible difference can it make whether we arrive together at my father's apartment, or if I'm already there and you come afterwards?'

Luke poured two drinks from the decanter, then turned and handed her one. His eyes were dark and implacable, and she felt this was one argument he had no intention of permitting her to win.

'Your father's dinner parties are his own affair,' he began with assumed indolence. 'We will accept his invitation but I will not have you take responsibility for the preparations. Is that understood?'

'You're being chauvinistic, *and* deliberately difficult!'

One dark eyebrow rose slightly. 'Chauvinistic?'

She flashed him an angry look that had no effect whatever. 'You'd allow me to prepare dinner for your —*our*,' she amended with emphasis, 'guests. But not for my father. Well,' she declared with renewed determination. 'I don't see how you can stop me.'

'No?'

The silky query raised a shiver of apprehension. As an opponent, Luke was infinitely formidable. 'What will you do—lock me in my room?' she countered defiantly.

'If you insist on behaving like a child, be warned that you will be treated accordingly.'

'Oh? What's that supposed to mean? Sent to bed with no dinner—or perhaps you'll forbid me to view television for a week?'

Luke's gaze was sardonic. 'None of those,' he dismissed cynically. 'My hand in hurtful contact with your elegantly-shaped derriere. Be sure of it, Sally,' he warned hardly.

She didn't doubt that he meant it—oh, he was hateful! 'If you so much as touch me, I—I'll——'

Suddenly he was standing much closer than before, and Sally took a backward step. 'You have not finished your drink,' he indicated smoothly. 'Carlo will doubtless announce dinner in a matter of minutes. A pity to waste such excellent sherry.'

'A change of subject won't change my mind,' she said stoically, and his lips twisted into a wry smile.

'The conversation is finished, *piccina*.'

'Oh, stop being so infernally patronising!' Sally burst out furiously. 'I'm a person in my own right. I won't be dictated to by a tyrannical husband. I *won't*!'

'Then be prepared to take the consequences, *mia sposa*.'

Deliberately, Sally drained the contents of her glass in one long swallow. 'I don't think I could bear to sit down at the same table with you. In fact, I'm not even hungry.'

'But you will eat,' Luke indicated dangerously. 'I shall insist on it.'

'Of course,' she said bitterly. 'I must be well fed with nourishing food—all the better to conceive the necessary *bambino*. One mustn't lose sight of my sole purpose as Luciano Andretti's wife.'

His eyelids drooped, partially screening his eyes, and for a moment Sally was vividly reminded of a jungle cat about to spring on an unwary prey. She watched in mesmerised facination as he reached out and placed the flat of his hand against her stomach. 'We have been married exactly one week—already you may be *incinta* with my son.'

'That you should be so fortunate!'

'Would you wish me a daughter?' he mocked, not removing his hand, and she wrenched away from his touch.

'If I could have my say, a whole bevy of daughters! But I shall pray for a son so that my debt is paid. Then I can escape,' she ended bitterly.

'Could you walk away from the child that has burgeoned inside your body until birth, then suckled at your breast?' he queried meaningfully. 'My child—but also *yours*? Allow it to grow up unseen, unaware of its childish triumphs and disappointments?'

Sally felt her eyes widen, mirroring the inner conflict his words aroused. She looked at him wordlessly, and was unable to utter a single sound. At last, after an interminable length of time, she managed to find her voice. 'Damn you, Luke Andretti,' she cursed shakily. 'Damn you to hell!' She turned and ran from

the room—at least, that was her intention, only a
steely grip on her arm halted her flight before she had
taken two steps. In a blaze of anger she swung back
to face him, and there were tears shimmering in her
eyes. 'I couldn't eat—the food would only stick in my
throat.'

'You will eat something, nonetheless.'

At the table in the dining-room she sat in stony
silence, taking only a spoonful or two of the *gazpacho*,
a morsel of veal *parmigiana*, leaving the side salad untouched, and she refused dessert. She did drink a
glass of wine, but that served only to make her feel
sleepy, and it was with infinite relief that she stood to
her feet at the end of the meal. The brief glance she
spared Luke revealed an expression deliberately bland
and enigmatic.

'I don't want any coffee,' she said quietly, moving
towards the door. She preceded Luke into the hallway,
then made her way past the lounge to the stairs, half
expecting him to stop her. He didn't, and she almost
ran upstairs in her hurry to get away from his hateful
presence.

In their bedroom the huge bed looked inviting, and
Sally sat down on its edge, feeling shaken and totally
bereft. She didn't know whether to weep or give way
to childish temper. His words kept echoing through
her brain, and she stretched out, sinking down into
the soft mattress with utter weariness.

She must have slept, although she had no recollection of drifting into that state. Her turbulent thoughts
seemed to extend into her subconscious mind, assum-
ing nightmarish proportion, so vivid as to be almost a
reality, and she wept, coming sharply awake at the
sound of her own voice.

The room was dark, and for a moment she had to

think where she was. With a hand that shook she reached out to switch on the bedside lamp, then buried her face in her hands.

The door swung open, and Luke stood in the aperture. 'In the name of heaven, what——' He moved into the room, then strode with measured steps to the bed. 'Sally, what is it, child?'

Sally shook her head, unwilling to admit her distress. 'Nothing. I had a dream, that's all.' She trembled violently as she felt the bed depress with his weight.

'From the sound of your scream, it was more nightmare than dream,' he determined grimly. 'You shall have some brandy.'

'I don't want anything,' she said wretchedly. 'Just go away and leave me alone.' She stood to her feet and crossed to the bathroom. A shower might shake off the strange wobbly sensation invading her limbs.

Ten minutes later she emerged into the bedroom, and came to an abrupt halt at the sight of Luke standing beside the bed, a half-filled tumbler of spirits in his hand. He had discarded his clothes, and his well-muscled frame was covered with a short towelling robe.

'I don't like brandy—it makes me cough,' she refused.

'Sip it, *piccina*,' he commanded quietly. 'It will help you sleep.'

'If I don't, I suppose you'll hold my nose and make me!'

A wry smile twisted his lips. 'Something like that.'

'You're a diabolical fiend, Luke Andretti!' The cry was one of anguish, and her eyes filled with frustrated tears.

'And a brute, eh?' he mocked cynically. 'Undoubtedly you wish you had never set eyes on me, let alone married——' He uttered a soft humourless laugh. 'Chained to the devil himself, are you not, *mia*?' He moved to stand beside her and held the glass to her lips. 'Sip it, *cara*,' he bade, 'until every drop has gone.'

His eyes forbade her to demur, and Sally took a few sips, then turned her face aside. 'I don't like the taste.'

'But it runs like warm fire through your veins, does it not? Come, a few drops more.' The glass tilted, and she sipped slowly, feeling a soft lethargy steal over her. 'Into bed, *piccina*.'

'I think you're a perfect——' She paused, unable to think of an adequate noun to describe him, and she was too bemused in an alcoholic mist to struggle when he lifted her into bed.

On the edge of sleep, she was vaguely aware of snuggling close against him as she pillowed her head on his chest, curious that she should feel both safe and secure in the arms of a man she professed to hate.

CHAPTER SIX

IT was just as well she had bought a new evening gown, Sally determined as she donned the patterned off-the-shoulder ankle-length dress the following evening. Of voile, featuring small multi-coloured roses against a black background, it hugged her waist, then flared in softly-gathered flounces to her ankles. She executed a slow pirouette before the mirror and was well pleased with the effect, loving the feel of the delicate material as it floated about her limbs with every move she made.

The news that they were to dine out that evening had been divulged very much as an afterthought by Luke a few minutes prior to his departure for the squash courts early Saturday afternoon. It irked her somewhat that he hadn't asked if she would like to accompany him, for squash was a game she enjoyed, and she would have relished pitting her skills against those of his—not that she expected to win, but the exercise would have proved a satisfying outlet.

Now, she carefully applied eye-shadow and mascara, coloured her lips and added a touch of lip-gloss, then examined her hair. Upswept on top of her head, or left loose? Perhaps a compromise, she pondered thoughtfully, swirling a thick swathe of hair into a carelessly-contrived knot on top of her head. There, that looked casually elegant, and went rather well with the style of her gown. A few dabs of perfume, and she was ready. The black cobwebby shawl lay on the bed, together with her evening bag.

'I will be accused of cradle-snatching,' Luke's voice drawled from the doorway, and Sally turned slowly to face him, a silent query arching her eyebrows.

'You look barely seventeen,' he explained dryly, and she retaliated with faint mockery.

'And never been kissed?'

'Your tongue has a sharp edge, *piccina*—could it be that I am at fault in some way?' He strolled into the room with the ease and assurance of a jungle cat, looking darkly handsome in a formal black suit that contrasted sharply with his immaculate white silk shirt.

'Did you enjoy your afternoon?' she parried, and heard his soft laugh.

'Ah, so that is it, hmm? I did not realise you were so anxious for my company.'

'I'm not,' she responded hastily, and deliberately crossed to the bed to collect her shawl and evening bag. 'I would have enjoyed a game—although not necessarily against you.'

'Afraid I might beat you?'

Sally shot him a withering glance. 'You have the distinct advantage of added height and strength—what chance would I have?'

Luke's eyes gleamed with humour. 'So you play the game too,' he mused. 'Very well, *cara*, we shall oppose one another—tomorrow afternoon?'

'Why not?' she accepted lightly, cherishing the thought that he was in for a surprise. Victory would be his—but not easily won, she'd make sure of that if she could!

The restaurant was exclusive and luxurious, and one to which Sally had not previously been escorted. They were joined within ten minutes by three other couples, and she found their company pleasant, the flow of conversation easy to maintain.

The meal was excellent, although Sally found it difficult to refrain from analysing each course, and she would have given much to discover the chef's recipe for *moussaka*. There was a subtle difference, a variation she had hitherto not experimented with, that added a piquant flavour to the dish.

Luke was at his most urbane, adopting the cloak of sophistication with utmost ease, and for a moment Sally viewed him with the eyes of a stranger. The discovery that she found him likeable was almost ludicrous, and yet there was a part of her that wished they were meeting for the first time—without the prickling resentment and the dislike she harboured against him. Would it make any difference? Decry it as she might, there was an indefinable pull—a charge of emotions that ran like liquid fire between them. She could hate him with every nerve in her body, but he had only to touch her and she was lost. It was almost as if she were two people inside one skin—one to hate, one to love. A taunting thought teased her brain. What would it be like to be loved and adored by Luke Andretti? Dear Lord—the wine must be going straight to her head!

'Dance with me, *cara*.'

Sally looked up, her lips parting with surprise as she saw Luke standing beside her, a strangely gentle smile curving his mouth, and she stood to her feet, not questioning her motives for placing her hand in his and following him on to the dance floor.

They didn't exchange a word, but it was almost as if there was a sudden merging of spirits that would have made conversation an intrusion. She felt his lips brush her temple, and it wasn't imagination that his arms tightened fractionally.

It wasn't until later that harsh reality brought her down to earth with a crashing thud, and afterwards

Sally wondered whether fate was responsible for choosing that precise moment in urging her towards the powder-room. A few more minutes and she would not have encountered Chantrelle, the only other occupant, calmly tidying her hair before the large mirror.

'Well, just look who's here, *and* looking quite starry-eyed into the bargain!' Chantrelle trilled brittlely. 'I've had my eyes on you for the past two hours, yet I doubt you've even noticed me. Philip is positively seething with frustrated jealousy.'

Sally felt her heart sink. Of all the luck, with the vast number of restaurants in Sydney, they had to choose the same one! 'The lighting is fairly dim, Chantrelle,' she suggested evenly.

'Enjoying married life, are you, dear? With a virile man such as Luke for a husband, you should be.' She uttered a harsh laugh, and cast Sally a pitying glance. 'Quite a coincidence, isn't it, how your father's business has made such a remarkable recovery? You were all set to become a modern-day Cinderella—then, hey presto, along came a fairy-tale prince to the rescue! Ah—but then you weren't suffering the delusion that Luke married you for love, surely?'

Sally felt her temper begin to rise. Calm, she must remain calm. The other girl's invective was deliberately designed to make her angry, and there was no way she would allow Chantrelle that satisfaction.

'You seem overly concerned with something that involves only Luke and myself,' she managed lightly.

'He's too much of a man for a child like you to handle,' Chantrelle declared disparagingly. 'A few weeks, a month maybe, and he'll become bored—then he'll begin seeking solace elsewhere.'

'You hope with you?'

Chantrelle returned her attention to the mirror and

carefully scrutinised her reflection. 'Doesn't it bother
you that there have been a long line of women in
Luke's life?'

Sally felt she had had enough. 'Why should it?' she
queried with amazing calm considering her inner turmoil. 'He married me. That should be self-explanatory,
surely?' She ignored Chantrelle, deliberately shutting
her ears to the derisive laugh as the other girl swept
past.

Sally took unnecessarily long attending to her
toilette, for in truth her hands shook with anger so
that her lipstick had to be reapplied twice. Her eyes
were stormy, and her smile when she practised it was
sadly lacking.

The noise of muted chatter and background music
served to lighten her features somewhat, and she was
halfway back to their table when a hand caught her
arm, bringing her to a halt.

'Sally!' The low-pitched voice reached her ears, and
she cast a startled glance at the owner, unable to believe that Philip had the gall to seek her out. His face
was an eloquent mask, and she had to school her
features into politeness.

'Hello, Philip. Is there something you wanted?'

'Why did you do it—in the name of God, why?' he
groaned urgently. 'You must have known I'd have
helped you, given time to think things over.'

Sally looked at him carefully, seeing the visible
signs of weakness in his too-handsome face, and wondered why she hadn't noticed them before. Compared
with Luke, Philip resembled an indecisive, insecure
youth. She winced slightly as his grip on her arm increased in pressure.

'Can't we meet somewhere—lunch, maybe? We've
things we must discuss.' He glanced round the

crowded room, then drew her closer towards him. 'Perhaps we should dance—it would look better.'

She tried to extricate her arm without success. 'I don't want to dance, thank you,' she refused with icy politeness. In a minute she'd explode! Really, he was unbelievable. 'And I have absolutely no intention of meeting you anywhere.'

'I go nearly crazy,' Philip muttered huskily, 'thinking about you in his arms, *his* bed. You don't know what you do to a man, Sally.' He bent close and his breath fanned the tendrils of hair that curled low on her neck. 'Leave him, I beg of you. Whatever——'

'If you don't let go of me this instant, I'll slap you,' she promised evenly.

'Why, you—*bitch*! I'd like to——'

'Another word, Mannering——' a voice warned with dangerous softness, and Sally's eyes flew sideways to catch sight of Luke standing less than a foot away. His expression was an enigmatic mask, but his eyes held an angry glitter she found positively frightening.

'Sally and I were just talking,' Philip blustered, and Luke raised an enquiring eyebrow.

'What I overheard could scarcely be deemed polite conversation,' he alluded cynically.

Philip went an unbecoming red, and ventured sullenly, 'I love her, dammit!'

'What makes you think *I* do not?' Luke queried silkily.

'You have a certain reputation, Andretti,' the other accused in a ugly tone.

'Indeed?' Luke's eyebrow rose sardonically, then he took Sally's arm. 'Excuse us, Mannering.'

'I imagine you could do with a drink?' Luke said coolly as they neared their table.

'A large one,' Sally agreed shakily as she followed him through the mingling crowd of diners. To be confronted first by Chantrelle, and then Philip, had been an unnerving experience. That Philip, of all people, should have revealed such nastiness was beyond her.

As much as she tried, Sally found it difficult to join in the lighthearted chatter exchanged by the occupants at their table for the remainder of the evening. She danced with each of the three men, and more than once with Luke, but she couldn't help feeling relieved when they made a move to leave.

It was shortly after one o'clock when the car drew to a halt in the garage, and she followed Luke into the house in silence. There wasn't a thing she could think of to say, any pleasantries with regard to enjoying the evening would verge on the banal.

'How well do you know Mannering?'

Sally started with surprise and almost missed her footing on the stairs. 'I didn't realise you knew Philip.'

'I am acquainted with his father,' Luke informed her dryly. 'And you did not answer my question.'

'I dated him for almost two years,' she revealed with a sigh of resignation.

'He seemed to think he had some prior claim.'

'Oh, for heaven's sake!' she cried in sudden anguish. 'What is this—some sort of inquisition? What do you want from me?' She rounded on him, her eyes brilliant with anger. 'He wanted to marry me. Is that enough?'

His eyes held a brooding indolence that was disquieting. 'I take it you did not want to marry him?'

'No!' Sally blazed. 'Damn your arrogance! What would you do if I demanded to know of your innumerable affairs? Carmela appears to be one of them! And Chantrelle made it quite plain she expects you to seek her favours when you become bored with me.' She turned away and began walking quickly down the hall towards their room. 'I'm "too much of a child to handle you"!' she flung over her shoulder as she opened the bedroom door, then in a fit of pique, she slammed it shut with a resounding clunk.

Without stopping, she crossed to the bed and flung off her shawl, feeling sick and disillusioned. She gave an inelegant sniff and tried to blink back the self-pitying tears that threatened to spill over and run down her cheeks.

'You seem to have taken particular exception to Chantrelle's remarks,' Luke declared ruminatively, coming into the room and closing the door behind him.

'How do you expect me to feel?' she uttered with hurt indignation. 'First Chantrelle, then Philip. And as if that isn't enough, you—you—— Oh! I *hate* men who fight over a woman,' she choked, 'like—like a pair of roosters fighting over a prized hen!'

His soft chuckle was her undoing, and she spun round to rail furiously,

'What kind of person are you?'

'A mere man, *piccina*,' he mocked lightly. 'What other label would you hang around my neck?'

'That of an inveterate rake!'

'With scores of women at my beck and call?'

'You're no monk,' Sally snapped, sorely tried, and caught his twisted smile.

'Would you prefer it if I were?'

'I couldn't imagine you ever taking vows of celibacy,' she observed with marked sarcasm.

'That observation conjures up a long line of women, when there really have not been all that many.'

'I find that difficult to believe.'

Suddenly he was standing directly in front of her and there was little she could do about the erratic thudding of her heart. 'You bear my name, Sally,' he remonstrated gently as his hands curved over her shoulders.

'You say it as if it's a medal I should wear with honour.'

'Poor *nina*.' He pulled her towards him, and she struggled to escape his hold.

'Please,' she protested. 'I want to go to bed.'

'So you shall,' he accorded wickedly, and a blush stole over her cheeks.

'Luke—please, don't——'

'Do not—what, *cara*?' he teased as his lips trailed her brow, then travelled with studied slowness down to seek the throbbing pulse at the base of her throat.

'Stop it,' she begged, a husky note entering her voice. In another minute she wouldn't be able to prevent her arms from sliding up around his neck.

'You feel it, too—this strange magical chemistry. Like the pull of a magnet drawing us together. Yet you ask me to stop?' he mocked, and his lips traced a fiery path up to the edge of her mouth to linger disturbingly until she ached for more than that light tantalising touch.

A tiny moan escaped her throat as she gave up trying to remain passive in his arms. Without conscious thought her mouth moved fractionally so her lips met his, and she was uncaring of the fervour with which she returned his kisses.

The following days passed without mishap, and scarcely an argument. Not that there was much opportunity to argue, Sally determined with a certain wryness, for Luke left early each morning for the city and returned in the evening. After a leisurely dinner he inevitably retired to the study, and she was left to view television or read.

On reflection, the days were enjoyably spent. Midweek saw most of the Christmas shopping completed, and she took pleasure in wrapping all the presents, especially those for Luke's two nephews and tiny niece. Added to which, she had shopping of her own, presents for her father, and for Luke. There were endless cards to write, so that the hours were never enough before she needed to begin preparations for the evening meal. Carlo had gracefully acceded to her suggestion that she prepare dinner each evening, for they had struck up an easy friendship, exchanging recipes and discussing food as if they'd known each other for years instead of mere weeks.

Thursday's evening meal was especially planned— not for any particular reason other than that Sally felt inclined to exercise her culinary talent to its fullest extent. Pasta, homemade that morning for the *spaghetti alla bolognese*, to be followed by *pollo sorpresa*, with a raspberry bombe for dessert. The preparations took most of the afternoon, and she was well pleased with the way things were progressing when Carlo entered the kitchen.

'Luke has just telephoned,' he began regretfully, 'and he wishes me to explain that something has come up which requires his personal attention, and therefore he will not be home for dinner. He sends his apologies.'

Sally couldn't explain the inexplicable disappointment she felt. She'd been looking forward to their shared evening meal, hopeful that it would follow the pattern of the previous three evenings when Luke had expressed pleasure with the food and exchanged light conversation.

'I guess we'll have a feast all to ourselves,' she managed with a smile, only to see him shake his head.

'You have forgotten, of course, but I have tonight off. It is the reunion I mentioned, if you remember? However, if you wish, I will stay.'

'I wouldn't hear of it,' Sally refused at once. 'I'll simply finish cooking, then when it's cooled I'll put it in the refrigerator. We'll reheat it tomorrow evening.'

Carlo frowned, his pleasant features creasing in contemplation. 'Are you not dining out?'

How could she forget? Tomorrow evening was her father's dinner party, and she was preparing the food. 'Never mind,' she shrugged lightly. 'I'll freeze it all, and no harm done.'

Carlo departed shortly after five, and at five-thirty the telephone rang. Sally answered it, hoping Luke had had a change in plan, only to discover that it was Carmela Ortega on the line. She had, she explained, missed Luke at the office, and was anxious to contact him. Sally politely informed her that Luke would not be home until late, but a message could be left. Carmela refused, explaining with immense pleasure, Sally felt sure, that it could wait until they met later that evening.

Sally replaced the receiver with controlled fury. So much for Luke's explanation—something personal requiring his attention, indeed!

Without further thought Sally dialled her father's apartment.

'Daddy, you're home,' she greeted without preamble, giving him no time to speak as soon as he answered. 'I have the most delicious dinner all ready to serve and no one to share it with. Set the table, and before you know it, I'll be there.' She replaced the receiver, then set about transferring the contents of saucepans into containers that could easily be carried to the car.

Fifteen minutes later she set the carton down on to the table in her father's dining-room, and began unloading its contents.

'To what do I owe this honour?' Joe Ballinger teased gently. 'It isn't my birthday, and Christmas isn't until next week.'

Sally cast him a wry smile. 'Don't ask me why—just sit down and enjoy it.'

'Let me guess. Luke rang at the last moment and said he wouldn't be home for dinner?'

'Right first time,' she answered lightly. 'So here I am. I even brought the wine.' She held a bottle aloft, then placed it on the table. 'Open it, Daddy. It's a particularly good claret, and will go rather well with the spaghetti.'

'Had your first quarrel, my dear?' Joe probed quietly, shooting her a particularly searching glance, and Sally managed a convincing smile as she shook her head.

'Heavens, no.' If he knew *how* many arguments they had——! 'You know my penchant for cooking,' she relayed with a negligent shrug. 'It's Carlo's evening off, and here I was with all this beautiful food and no one to share it with. I immediately thought of you,' she finished quizzically, and Joe laughed.

'I'm convinced, Sally. Let's eat.'

The time simply flew as they talked, and it was almost ten by the time the dishes were done and she was ready to leave. True, she did experience a faint feeling of unease that she'd left no note for Luke as to her whereabouts, but the feeling was shortlived as she garaged the car.

The Alfa-Romeo was not in its customary place, and she entered the house feeling vaguely resentful that he was not yet home.

After returning the saucepans and various containers to their rightful place in the kitchen, Sally filled the kettle with the intention of making some coffee, then when it was made she took it through to the *salotto* and switched on the television.

'Dutifully waiting for my return, *mia sposa*?'

Sally swung her head in the direction of Luke's mocking drawl, and restrained the impulse to burst into angry accusatory speech. 'Good heavens, no,' she managed with contrived indifference, and saw him smile.

'A good programme?'

'Very.'

'You have been watching it for some time?'

Something in his tone warned her not to prevaricate. He had no way of knowing she hadn't been home all evening—unless he'd telephoned. She pushed back a stray lock of hair, and met his gaze unwaveringly. 'About twenty minutes. Did you enjoy your dinner?' She tried to make the query sound casual, but obviously didn't succeed, for he quirked an eyebrow and countered smoothly,

'Do I detect a note of censure, *piccina*?'

Sally glanced back towards the television. 'You're imagining things. I couldn't care less where you spend your evenings, or with whom,' she ended coolly, and didn't hear his soft footfalls on the carpet as he crossed the room.

'My "evening" was solely business,' Luke drawled with imperturbable calm from somewhere close behind her, and she gave an undisguised sigh of exasperation.

'Of course! Carmela hinted otherwise when she rang after failing to catch you at the office. However——' she paused, adding with deliberate sarcasm, 'She declined to leave a message as she would be able to deliver it personally when she met you for dinner.'

'I could almost imagine you to be jealous. Are you, *piccina*?'

'No!' she denied emphatically. 'Although next time you decide not to come home for dinner, let me know in advance so that I'll be spared unnecessary time preparing a meal.'

'What gastronomical delight did I forsake?'

Oh, his sardonic amusement was infuriating! 'Nothing special, I assure you!' She stood to her feet in one fluid movement. 'I'm going to bed.'

Luke stepped sideways and effectively blocked her path. 'Not so fast,' he berated softly. 'Carmela, for all that she is a woman, is a highly qualified accountant. We work together on occasion, and when we cannot meet during conventional business hours, we usually elect to share a dinner table.' He leant out a hand to touch her hair, and Sally jerked away. 'You have no reason to be jealous.'

'I am not *jealous*! You can have dinner with a hundred different women on a hundred different nights, for all I care. I'd rather not be confronted with them, that's all,' she declared unevenly, and he broke into throaty laughter, querying wickedly,

'I am to be discreet, is that it?' He caught the hand she swung up towards his face. 'Oh no, my little fury,' he murmured softly, pulling her effortlessly forward. 'Now tell me why you were not here when I rang—twice, during the course of the evening?'

Sally tried to pull away without success. She wanted to beat her fists against his broad chest in sheer frustrated rage. 'It seemed a shame to let the food I'd cooked go to waste, so I rang Daddy and took everything there. Why? Did you think I had an assignation with another man?'

Luke's eyes narrowed fractionally. 'You possess a careless tongue,' he commented dryly. 'Be warned that if I so much as suspected——' His voice trailed off silkily, and Sally felt a shiver slide down her spine. For a long moment he looked down at her, then he released her hands. 'Go to bed, Sally. I will be up later.'

Sally escaped, taking the stairs two at a time in places, employing such haste that the devil himself could have been at her heels, and when she reached their room she peeled off her clothes and slipped beneath the shower.

Sleep wasn't an easy captive, and she lay awake for what seemed an age before she began to feel pleasantly drowsy. It was almost an anti-climax when Luke entered the room, and she lay still, tensing for the moment when he would join her. When his even breathing indicated that he had fallen asleep, she told herself she was glad—yes, *glad*, that he hadn't reached out to claim her, but her traitorous body had a will of its own, and she lay awake for a long time before tiredness finally claimed her.

CHAPTER SEVEN

WHEN Sally woke next morning it was late, and Luke had already left for the city. Not that she would have wished to face him, for she wasn't sure she was capable of uttering a civil word.

As the day progressed, she became entirely caught up with preparations for her father's dinner party. Firstly, there was the shopping, which took most of the morning, then she had a hurried lunch and drove to her father's Rose Bay apartment.

It was almost like old times being in the familiar kitchen, and alone, she could almost forget she was Sally Andretti, and imagine that her marriage, and even Luke himself, were part of a fantasy.

The menu she had chosen was elaborate, and the preparations took unlimited time, so that it was almost four o'clock before she realised Luke was unaware of her whereabouts. A cold hand momentarily clutched at her stomach as she envisaged his reaction. He had been adamant a week ago that she was to have nothing to do with the preparations, and the subject hadn't arisen since then. Quite what he would do when he discovered she had defied him didn't bear thinking about.

Her brain whirled. She'd ring home, and leave a message with Carlo. Yes, that was by far the better idea. To contemplate telephoning Luke at his office was definitely inadvisable, and she didn't even consider it.

At five-thirty the shrimp cocktail was arranged in

individual glass dishes, the fillet of beef *en cochonailles* was browning in the oven, the bearnaise sauce prepared and ready, and the lemon meringue pie for dessert was cooling on the bench.

She had time for a quick shower, then she'd change into the clothes she'd brought to wear this evening. Quickly she effected her toilette, then donned the flounced skirt in jersey-silk with pale beige flowers printed against a charcoal background. With it she wore a blouse of matching beige, and pinned on a charcoal-coloured artificial rose. Slender-heeled black strappy shoes completed the outfit, and she was well pleased with the effect. Make-up was kept to a minimum and there was little time to do anything much with her hair. After several hard strokes of the brush she left it loose to fall around her shoulders.

Sally emerged into the lounge just as the front door opened admitting her father, and she crossed to greet him, a smile lighting her features into something quite beautiful.

'My dear, you look ravishing,' Joe complimented sincerely as he gave her an affectionate hug. 'Marriage certainly agrees with you.' He shrugged off his jacket, then sniffed appreciatively. 'Ah—that aroma. Now, let me guess——' he paused, then ventured tentatively, 'Beef—with bearnaise sauce. Am I right?'

She chuckled and put her head to one side. 'One day I'll confound you with something quite undetectable. Shall I fix you a drink?'

'I'll get *you* one,' Joe insisted, and she smiled.

'Well, I still have the coffee tray to prepare. Bring your drink and mine into the kitchen so we can talk.'

'What time do you expect Luke to arrive?'

Sally considered the question thoughtfully, then managed to convey an answer that was evasive. 'He rarely arrives home before six. He'll want to shower and shave. Around seven, I'd say.'

Joe Ballinger smiled his approval. 'The others are coming just after seven. I thought we'd eat at seven-thirty.'

'Whenever you say,' she returned easily, moving in the direction of the kitchen, and after a few minutes he entered with a glass of sherry held in each hand.

'You didn't tell me who the guests are to be,' she queried, and saw him shake his head.

'My dear—how remiss of me! The Nordesteins, of course. The Bakersfields, Chantrelle and some young man. Andrea swore her daughter would be devastated not to be included,' he twinkled amusingly. 'Then there are the Engels, and—let me see, yes, the Burts. That's it.'

Chantrelle—she would have to come, wouldn't she? Sally fretted silently. She wouldn't bring Philip, surely? Sally dismissed that idea almost as soon as it came to mind as being quite improbable.

At precisely seven o'clock the doorbell chimed, and Joe went to answer it, ushering in the Nordesteins, who were quickly followed by the Burts, then the Engels. Charles and Andrea Bakersfield brought up the rear, and soon the lounge was nicely crowded. There was only Chantrelle and her partner to arrive —and *Luke*.

Where was he, for heaven's sake? Sally felt an edge of doubt begin to gnaw at her composure, making her vague and lacking in concentration. Perhaps he wouldn't come. Oh God—no matter how angry he was, he wouldn't not show up, surely?

Her nerves shredded at the sound of the doorbell, and try as she might her smile was a facsimile of gaiety when Chantrelle entered the lounge with a strange man in tow.

The muted peal of the telephone reached her ears, and she forced herself to sip her sherry slowly. The desire to toss it back was almost irresistible. She saw her father reach for the receiver, then speak, and after a few seconds of silence he appeared to smile.

In mesmerised fascination she watched him cross the room to her side.

'That was Luke,' he intimated quietly. 'He's just leaving Vaucluse now. Apparently he's been delayed in the city.'

The relief was extraordinary. However, as the time of his arrival drew close Sally became jittery, and was unable to stop her gaze swivelling towards the front door at ten-second intervals. Finally she could stand it no longer, and made her escape to the kitchen on the pretext of checking the vegetables.

Five minutes later some sixth sense warned her she was being watched, and she turned slowly, raising her head to meet the dark enigmatic gaze of her husband.

'Have you been given a drink?' What a ridiculous thing to say—he had one in his hand! Oh, why didn't he say something—anything would be better than this awful silence.

'You elected to disregard my wishes, I see,' Luke observed in a silky voice, and she suppressed a shiver of apprehension. 'Orders, don't you mean?' She ran a shaky hand through her hair, then ran the tip of her tongue nervously along her lower lip. What was wrong with her, for heaven's sake? Where was the customary anger he invariably managed to arouse? She should be feeling triumphant at having flouted him, but instead she felt incredibly forlorn.

Luke moved into the room, his movements deliberately controlled. 'I prefer to term them other-wise.'

'I refuse to be intimidated,' she issued quietly. 'And I'd prefer not to argue with you—at least, not here.'

'In that case, I suggest you come into the lounge and share a drink with me, and endeavour to play the adoring wife,' he declared dryly, and Sally was unable to refrain from querying,

'While you take the part of a devoted husband?'

He stepped close and caught hold of her chin. 'Careful, *piccina*,' he warned. 'Do not ignite the fuse to my temper.'

Sally looked at him wordlessly, and felt her lips tremble beneath his raking scrutiny. A brief hard kiss bruised her mouth, then she was free.

'If you look at me like that, *cara*,' Luke drawled, 'it will be thought I beat you into submission.'

'Can you deny that you don't intend to?' she countered shakily, and saw his lips twist into a mocking smile as he suggested smoothly,

'Let us join your father's guests.' Taking hold of her elbow he led her out into the lounge, refilling her glass with solicitous care.

Everyone in the room seemed to be smiling, and conscious that she was supposed to be an ecstatically happy bride, Sally attempted to play the part. With Luke at her side she circled the room, introducing him with seeming adoration to her father's friends. When they reached Chantrelle, Sally's smile was falsely bright.

'There's no need for introductions, darling. Luke and I are old friends,' the other girl declared sunnily. 'Philip declined gracefully—and who could blame him?' She indicated the man at her side with a careless hand. 'This is Gavin Sanderson, one of my father's colleagues.'

'A rather junior underling,' Gavin corrected. He appeared genuinely friendly, and Sally uttered a light laugh in response to his warm smile.

'I'm surprised you didn't arrive together,' Chantrelle commented, deliberately barbing her words, and Luke offered in smooth explanation,

'Sally wished to assist with dinner preparations.'

'Of course—Sally cooked for a living, didn't she? Forgive me for not remembering,' Chantrelle replied tritely, which was a definite falsehood considering the number of dinners she'd enjoyed as Joe Ballinger's guest, Sally perceived.

'They say that the way to a man's heart is through his stomach,' Chantrelle continued idly, shooting Luke a look that was openly suggestive. 'I presume Sally does possess other talents?'

Luke gave a light chuckle, then much to Sally's chagrin he caught her hand and lifted it to his lips. His eyes sparkled down at her with studied intimacy as he kissed her fingers before letting his lips caress the palm of her hand. 'I am totally bewitched,' he said softly.

'My, my—Sally must let me have the secret of her success,' Chantrelle drawled with thinly veiled sarcasm. 'Philip is certainly besotted,' she revealed sweetly, her head to one side. 'But a hardened cynic such as you, Luke, I would have thought to be immune from the tactics of a pretty little blonde.'

Sally writhed inwardly. If they weren't in her father's apartment, and she wasn't responsible for dinner, she'd give voice to a few uncharitable remarks! Aloud, she said with seeming sweetness, 'Perhaps Luke wanted a trained chef, and decided to combine my talents in that direction with a wedding ring,' she suggested with mock-humour, darting a provocative glance upwards, and on meeting the warning evident in those dark eyes she reached up and touched his lips with a careless finger. 'Don't look so fierce, darling—I was only teasing.'

'I'm sure Luke doesn't care whether you can cook or not,' Gavin intervened, and Sally warmed to him. At least he seemed to be an ally in this verbal war with Chantrelle.

'If you'll excuse me, I shall see about serving dinner,' she said aloud, and extricating her hand from Luke's clasp she made her escape.

To say the evening was an unqualified success would have been an exaggeration, for even the most undiscerning person would have been aware of the undercurrent of dislike Chantrelle directed towards Sally.

It was all Sally could do to retain a sense of politeness, and when they had all vacated the dining-room for the lounge she breathed a sigh of relief. At least now she was no longer confined to the table, and she could circulate among the guests.

'You really can cook. That was a fantastic meal.'

Sally turned to see Gavin Sanderson at her side, and she gave an appreciative smile. 'Thank you, I'm glad you enjoyed it.'

'I gather you've only recently married?'

He was quite charming—and much too nice for Chantrelle! 'A few weeks—two, to be exact.'

'Lucky Luke,' he said lightly. 'If you weren't married, I'd ask you for a date. I don't suppose—no,' he shook his head, smiling slightly, and she gave an answering smile.

'You're right, I wouldn't,' she said quietly. 'Have

you known Chantrelle long?'

'Long enough. Does that answer your question?'

It did, in more ways than one, Sally perceived. Her eyes glided idly round the room and lighted on Luke having what appeared to be a serious conversation with her father. She watched as Chantrelle joined the two men, then moments later Charles Bakersfield interrupted them and drew Joe Ballinger to one side. Her heart did a series of somersaults as Chantrelle placed her hand on Luke's arm, and the little green monster rose unbidden to the fore. How dare she! Twin flags of colour lit Sally's cheeks, and the blue of her eyes became intensified as she caught the intimate smile Chantrelle directed up at Luke.

All of a sudden she became aware of Gavin's voice, and she said distractedly, 'I'm sorry—what did you say?'

'I vote for breaking up that twosome,' Gavin declared musingly, offering her his arm. 'Shall we?'

Sally accorded him a wicked grin. 'Definitely!'

It was impossible to determine much from Luke's expression—he could have been bored, or enthralled. His eyes seemed to assume a quizzical gleam as she reached him, and one arm lifted to settle round her shoulders, drawing her close to his side.

It seemed perfectly natural to stand here like this, Sally thought silently. There was a warmth, a feeling of belonging she had not hitherto experienced—almost as if this large-framed man was a part of her, linked by destiny. Strange, she mused, I should hate him— in fact, I thought I did. But now——

'Do you intend coming back from wherever you have been for the past few minutes?' a voice teased close to her ear, and she lifted eyes bright with confusion to meet Luke's faintly amused expression. She coloured slightly at Gavin's open smile—Chantrelle's expression defied description!

'I'm sorry.' She attempted a shaky laugh, and glanced up at Luke. 'I was miles away.'

'Sally,' Joe Ballinger interrupted, 'there's a call for you from New York. You'd better take it in my study.'

New York! 'Mother?' she queried in disbelief. *Emily?*

'The very same,' her father confirmed dryly. 'I've already spoken to her, and now it's your turn.'

Good grief! Her mother always did have a zany sense of timing!

'Off you go. I'll send Luke in for moral support in about five minutes.' His eyes twinkled wickedly down at his daughter, and she gave him a sheepish grin.

'The inestimable Emily Breckenridge-Browning. Wish me luck!'

The line was remarkably clear. Emily could have been in the same room. Sally clutched the receiver and tried not to smile, as after an initial greeting her mother came straight to the point.

'What is all this nonsense in your letter about being married?'

'Nonsense, Mother?'

'Who is he, this man? Andretti—that's Italian, isn't it? What, Sally, are you doing married to an Italian?' Emily's voice rose incredulously, and Sally hid a grin.

'Daddy approves of him,' she said mildly.

'Your father never did have any sense!' Emily discounted. 'Why wasn't I informed? I am your mother, after all. And why such a hurried affair? You're not——?' the unspoken query hung suspended in the air.

'Pregnant? It's possible, but not probable,' Sally answered impishly.

'I suppose he's some pauperish immigrant. I shan't rest until I've seen what you've got yourself into,' Emily's voice wailed. 'You've certainly inherited your father's instincts—you never did take after me. Is he?'

'Is he—what, Mother?' She looked up as Luke came into the study, and she gave him a wry smile.

'Sally! Aren't you listening to me at all? Is this—man—an immigrant? Has he any money?'

'Yes, to both questions.'

'Is he there with you? Is that why you're being evasive?'

Sally covered the mouthpiece, and her eyes positively sparkled. 'I think it's time you met your mother-in-law—long-distance.' She beckoned Luke forward, while into the receiver she said brightly, 'Mother, Luke is standing beside me. Would you like to speak to him?'

'I presume he speaks English—oh drat, Sally, I probably won't understand a word he says!'

Sally handed Luke the receiver mutely, her eyes alight with ill-concealed mirth.

It was all of five minutes before she took the receiver again. 'Mother? Daddy's giving a party right now—we should go. Besides, this call must be costing you a fortune.'

'What's money?' Emily queried blithely. 'I've decided I must see you, Sally. I'm not at all satisfied you haven't made some ghastly mistake. Your Luke sounds all right,' she conceded conservatively. 'However, voices can be deceiving. I shall catch the first available flight after New Year's Day. I trust there's a spare bedroom somewhere that I can have?'

Oh dear, this would never do at all! 'Mother——'

'Goodbye, darling,' Emily intervened smoothly. 'Go back to your party. Merry Christmas.'

The line went dead, and Sally slowly replaced the receiver. Her expression was a study of emotions as she looked across at Luke. 'Having spoken to Mother, you will soon experience the added pleasure of meeting her. She intends visiting us,' she concluded wryly.

'Your mother will, of course, be our guest,' Luke stated, and she chuckled as she cast sparkling eyes in his direction.

'I'm afraid you're going to be investigated to the nth degree. Will you mind?'

He gave a negligent shrug. 'It sounds very much as if I have little say in the matter.' He took hold of her arm and began leading her towards the door. 'Shall we return to your father's guests?'

Sally felt almost regretful at having to go back into the lounge, and on glancing up at Luke's rugged profile her eyes lingered on his mouth. It was quite crazy, but for a moment she wanted to have those firm lips touch hers. In mesmerised fascination she came to a halt.

'Are you pleading with me, *mia*?'

His softly-voiced query startled her, and she burst into confused speech. 'I—no, of course not.'

'A pity,' he accorded with a quizzical gleam, and Sally put a hand up to her hair in a purely nervous gesture.

'I must make some coffee. It's almost eleven o'clock.'

'I shall allow you to get away with it this time— however, later you will not escape so easily. If you remember, we have a score to settle.'

'You—wouldn't dare,' she choked in disbelief, 'lay a hand on me——'

'I do not make idle threats, *piccina*—you should know that. Now, let us go back to the lounge.'

'I hate you!' she flung in a helpless whisper, and

his cynical laugh only served to infuriate her.

'Not *all* of the time,' he mocked softly.

If anyone noticed anything amiss it would have been remarkable, Sally decided wryly, for Luke didn't move far from her side during the ensuing hour and a half, and he played the role of adoring husband to the hilt. Everyone, including her father, could not have doubted they were a loving couple. Chantrelle, who deserved top honours for trying, didn't get so much as a chance to inveigle Luke into more than the briefest of conversations, and he was at his most urbane. His arm shifted from around Sally's waist to rest lightly about her shoulders, then he caught hold of her hand and rubbed his thumb gently against the throbbing pulse at her wrist. She smiled, even laughed on occasion, and managed to make sophisticated conversation, but beneath it all she was seething with silent anger, and longed for the moment when they could leave.

At last there was a general exodus, and when the door closed on the last guest, Joe turned to Sally with an affectionate smile. 'We must endeavour not to let too much time go by before we get together again. Thank you, Sally, for a delectable dinner, and Luke, for allowing her to prepare it.' He waved a hand towards the tray of drinks. 'You'll join me in a nightcap? I have a bottle of Courvoisier cognac I've been saving for just such an occasion.'

'Thank you, Joe. Just a small one, then we must be on our way.' Luke wandered with leisurely strides across the room, drawing Sally along at his side, and she accepted a small quantity of cognac.

'Merry Christmas, Daddy,' she bade, raising her glass. 'And many more of them,' she added gently.

Joe acknowledged her words with a smile. 'I take

it you weren't able to dissuade Emily from crossing the Atlantic?'

'Not a chance! She's due to descend immediately after New Year.'

'I think,' her father twinkled unrepentantly, 'that I shall have urgent business in another State. After the initial confrontation, Luke may very well decide to join me.'

Sally gave a cry of mock-anguish. 'Don't you dare desert me! I shall be needing all the moral support I can get.'

'We have something like ten days in which to prepare some kind of strategy,' Joe murmured thoughtfully. 'When do you arrive back from Surfers' Paradise?'

'Tuesday week,' Luke affirmed. 'And, unless I am mistaken, I have to fly to Adelaide the following day.' He glanced down at Sally. 'How long is your mother likely to stay?'

'With us? A few days—a week, maybe,' she ventured. 'It's difficult to say. Emily has two sisters she'll want to visit while she's here, but they're in such far-flung places as Perth and Darwin.'

'In that case, it would be feasible for her to visit us first, then return for a few days before flying back to America,' he drawled.

Joe began to chuckle, and then finally burst into laughter. 'My dear ex-wife will undoubtedly do the unexpected. I learnt many years ago never to plan anything while Emily is anywhere in the vicinity.'

Luke drained the last of his cognac and replaced the glass. The glance he cast down at Sally held a certain warmth. 'Come, *piccina*, it is time we left.'

Oh, that mocking endearment was maddening! She decided to teach him a lesson, and standing on tiptoe she brushed her lips against his chin. 'Don't be in such a hurry, darling.' She gave the last word deliberate emphasis, and his husky laugh did little to help her composure.

'*Amante*,' he drawled, 'I am not in the least embarrassed at hurrying you home.'

A tide of colour flooded her cheeks, and even her father, whom she considered a faithful ally, deserted her in a moment of need.

'Away with you! I haven't forgotten what it's like to be newly married and in love.' Joe chuckled, and Sally could feel the laughter shake his chest as he hugged her close. 'Merry Christmas, honey. Take care!'

Sally stood in hostile silence as the elevator made its swift descent, and in the car she refused to look anywhere but at the road ahead.

'Are you not going to speak at all?' Luke queried musingly, and she was goaded into retorting,

'You're impossible! In fact, aside from Emily, whom I dearly love, you're the most impossible person I know!'

'And I, of course, am not fortunate enough to be loved.' His amusement was the very limit, and as soon as the car came to a standstill in the garage, Sally made haste to put as much distance as possible between them. Whatever was gained soon became lost as she was forced to wait until he unlocked the side door into the house, and then she wasn't permitted to escape. Her arm was grasped by hard fingers that tightened their grip painfully as she wrenched away, and she had little option but to climb the two flights of stairs at his side.

In the bedroom he set her free, and she stood facing him, infuriated beyond measure. 'Did you have to be so—frank, in front of my father? Have you no decency at all?' Her voice rose to a scandalised crescendo, and she stamped her foot in sheer frustration as a deep chuckle emerged from his throat. 'I know firsthand what a—a lusty—animal you are,' she breathed furiously, 'but do you have to make it so blatantly obvious?'

'I am at a loss to know why you should be so furious,' Luke drawled sardonically. 'As I recall, you enjoy my—er—lustiness——' He moved fractionally to one side as her hand swung up towards his face. 'Oh no, my little wildcat. I do not fight with women, and unless severely provoked, I rarely strike one. However, I am sorely tempted to make of you an exception,' he concluded, catching hold of her hands.

'If you so much as touch me, I'll never forgive you.' The last few words choked in her throat, and to her utter consternation angry tears welled up and spilled down her cheeks. She could only look at him wordlessly as she tried to wrench her hands out of his grasp. 'You're hurting me,' she whispered as his fingers tightened over the delicate bones of both wrists, and at once the pressure lessened.

'There are times when I could shake you until every bone rattles, such is the degree of anger you arouse,' he declared hardily, then he swore softly. '*Dio!* Your tears confound me! I have a girl-child on my hands who continually fights against becoming a woman. Why, *cara*? You are not averse to my lovemaking, so why create such a storm?'

Still he didn't free her hands, and she tentatively licked away a tear as it came to rest at the edge of her mouth. 'Our entire existence together, even your possession of me, has been stormy,' she said shakily.

'A stormy possession?' Luke drawled sardonically.

'Yes, it has been that. Shall we declare a truce?'

'Do you think we could get through a day without an argument?'

'When we rarely last more than an hour in each other's company without one?' he queried musingly. 'In thirty-six hours we leave to visit my sister. It means a great deal to me that Angelina be convinced of our happiness. Shall we agree not to differ for eight days?'

Sally swallowed painfully. 'As long as you don't become insufferably overbearing, it shouldn't be too difficult.'

Luke's smile became faintly cynical. 'Is that how you see me? You married a Latin, *mia sposa*. Despite many years in this country, I still retain many of the old ways.'

'A wife should be dutiful, subservient, and,' she declared broodingly, 'never argue with her husband. Unfortunately, I wasn't brought up with those ideals.' She looked up at him in all seriousness. 'We're bound to clash—I guess it's inevitable.'

'Perhaps,' he conceded thoughtfully. 'You can be dismayingly self-willed at times—this evening, for example.'

'Can't you understand?' she flashed quickly. 'It will be the first Christmas Daddy and I have spent apart, and besides, I've been preparing his dinner parties for years.'

'But he can no longer lay claim to your services in that direction.' Luke's eyes darkened fractionally. 'You cannot continue playing the role of his social hostess.'

'You expect it of me.'

'You are my wife.'

'Oh, there you go again!' she flung desperately. 'You assume a mantle of arrogance that commands blind obedience, and if I should dare to disobey, you think you have the right to mete out some form of punishment! Well, I refuse to be treated like some recalcitrant child!'

'And I , *cara*, will not tolerate———'

'*You* won't tolerate!' she exploded. 'On almost every occasion we've dined out I've come face to face with one of your—conquests. They seem to regard you as some prize I've snatched from beneath their very noses! How do you think it feels to know that they've known you———' she trailed off expressively. 'I pale into insignificance compared with their sophistication. I'm sure they are convinced you've fallen prey to some temporary form of amnesia by marrying me, and they're hanging in there like leeches for the moment you'll tire of your—innocent, boring little wife!'

'My dear Sally,' he murmured musingly, 'you are the antithesis of boring, and for someone who recently assured me she did not care if I took out a hundred different women you are showing quite remarkable jealousy.' He drew her close to look down at her with quizzical amusement. 'Would liking me—even loving me, be such a terrible cross to bear?'

'Yes! And I won't—ever!'

There was a sudden flaring of terrible anger in his eyes that frightened her. '*Madonna mia*,' he swore savagely, 'I begin to think there is only one way to silence you!'

The indignity of being flung face down across his powerful thigh was mortifying to say the least, and the slaps he rendered had a stinging quality that hurt abominably long after he'd stood her to her feet.

'Now you have reason to hate me. And be warned,' he threatened with ominous quietness. 'If you dare to provoke me again, I will not hesitate to repeat the spanking.'

As soon as the bathroom door closed behind him Sally gave in to the luxury of silent tears, and spent considerable time mulling vengefully on ways she could get back at him. Without qualification, he was the most tyrannical man she'd ever met! She sat down on the edge of the bed with care. Brute, she accused wrathfully, hating him with every nerve in her body. She'd never been so humiliated in her entire life! He was nothing but an arrogant, domineering—— Oh! For two pins she'd move into one of the spare bedrooms.

Even as the thought occurred, she was on her feet and slipping out of her clothes with speed, and in less than two minutes she was pulling on a robe over her nightgown.

In the hallway she took down sheets and a pillowcase from the linen closet.

'What do you think you are doing?'

Sally spun round and glared at Luke as he covered the distance between them. Her chin lifted defiantly. 'I'm going to sleep in one of the spare rooms.'

'The hell you are,' he said succinctly, and at once her eyes grew stormy, their blue becoming intensified as she vented her anger at him.

'If you think for one minute I'll submit to your love-making after—that——' she spluttered, and became totally infuriated when he took the linen from her hands and tossed it down on to the carpet. 'You're nothing but a sadistic brute, Luke Andretti!' she cried, flying at him to flail her fists against his chest until he forced her to stop.

'You are behaving like a spoilt child. Now, stop it, and come to bed.'

'I don't want to come to bed—at least, not with you.'

'You are not a very good liar, *piccina*,' he drawled, his eyes gleaming sardonically as they rested on her heaving bosom. They travelled with deliberate indolence to her mouth, and it was almost as if she could feel the tangible pressure of his lips on hers. Bending his head, he brushed his lips against her temple, then trailed them down to rest at the side of her throat where a rapidly-beating pulse revealed the true state of her emotions. Gently he nuzzled an earlobe, then his lips found hers in a kiss that rocked her very being.

Coherent thought became lost as she began drowning in the incredible ecstasy his touch evoked, and she was scarcely aware that he lifted her into his arms and carried her towards the bedroom.

CHAPTER EIGHT

Most of the passengers on the flight from Sydney to Brisbane appeared to be bursting with bonhomie, and doubtless the festive season was responsible.

Sally felt distinctly nervous as the jet touched down at Brisbane airport, and she followed Luke's broad frame across the tarmac with some trepidation. The thought of meeting his sister was daunting, although the children would provide plenty of distraction. Three under five years, and one a baby! Her lips curved into a winsome smile.

'There is Frank,' Luke declared, and Sally's eyes followed the direction of his outstretched arm.

It appeared that Angelina had elected to wait for them at home, rather than bring the children and thus strain the station-wagon to capacity, and during the hour-long drive from the airport to Surfers' Paradise Sally was able to discern that Luke fully approved of his brother-in-law, and what was more, they were firm friends.

Surfers' Paradise was essentially geared for the tourist industry, and high-rise hotels abounded along the shoreline. Scenically, it was idyllic. The ocean looked cool and inviting, the sea a deep translucent green that merged into blue, and breakers rolled inshore to crash softly, thrusting up white foamy spray. A colourful array of beach umbrellas lined the soft white sand, and throngs of minimally-clothed sun-loving tourists lay prone soaking up the warmth of the semi-tropical sun, which at the height of summer was particularly intense.

The station-wagon drew to a halt in the driveway outside a modern brick bungalow, and no sooner had they alighted than two small bundles of boyishly-clad humanity flung themselves helter-skelter at their uncle.

With a laugh Luke gathered them up together and buried his head between each of theirs. It was quite something to witness, and Sally felt the prick of emotional tears at the back of her eyes.

'So—you are Sally.'

She turned swiftly and met the dark eyes in the olive-complexioned features of the girl standing before her. In her late twenties, Angelina Forresto was startlingly attractive.

'Yes—and you have to be Angelina,' Sally returned, smiling at the baby perched on Luke's sister's hip. She was gorgeous, with huge dimples and a positively beauteous smile.

'Those two little terrors temporarily being models of good behaviour in Luke's arms are named Gianni and Luigi,' Angelina indicated with maternal pride. 'And this little angel is Lisa.'

Sally smiled as the two little boys' voices rose to an excited crescendo, and Angelina laughed.

'Let us go inside. Frank will bring the luggage.'

They entered a spacious lounge furnished with cane chairs and settees, on which brightly-patterned cushions lent colour that tastefully blended with cool green walls and polished wood floors. The house appeared quite large, Sally perceived as she followed Luke's sister down a wide hallway. There were four bedrooms, the last of which she was to share with Luke during their stay. There were rugs on the floor, colourful covers on both beds, and ample space for their clothes in the wardrobe.

'Hey, *amici*, down you go, hmm? As yet, I have not had a chance to say a word to your *mamma*.' Luke let them slide to the floor, then plucking the baby from his sister's arms he handed the little tot to Sally and greeted Angelina.

'Marriage suits you,' Angelina teased as she stood back to survey him critically, then she turned to Sally. 'I was beginning to despair that he would ever marry and become a papa to his own children. He is rather special, this brother of mine—you are a lucky girl.'

Sally's eyes twinkled wickedly as she looked across at Luke. 'I think he's special, too,' she affirmed with just the right amount of dreaminess in her voice.

'I could develop a swelled head from all this flattery,' Luke declared with a chuckle, and his sister laughed.

'I will leave you to change and unpack your things. Come into the lounge afterwards and we will have a drink before lunch.'

Sally eyed Luke a trifle warily as soon as the door shut. 'Your nephews quite obviously idolise you.'

'You find it difficult to comprehend that anyone could idolise me, *mia sposa*?'

'Oh, stop being so cynical,' she accused wryly, and cast a glance towards the two beds. 'Which bed will you have?'

His smile was infinitely mocking as he shrugged the jacket from his shoulders. 'My dear Sally, does it matter? I imagine we will use only one of them.'

'Oh, stop it!' she whispered angrily. 'I thought we were going to observe a truce.'

'I was merely teasing, *piccina*,' he drawled. 'In which suitcase have you hidden the children's presents? They are splendid, do you not think?'

'The presents or the children?' she queried, deliberately misunderstanding him, and as his eyes darkened fractionally she held up her hands in a gesture of defeat. 'All right, I'm sorry. I think the children are lovely—especially Lisa.' She couldn't resist a tiny smile. 'Those dimples! She's going to knock the boys for six when she's older.'

Luke clicked open one of the suitcases and began unfolding trousers, then shirts.

'I'll do that,' Sally remonstrated, crossing to his side. 'They'll crease if they're not hung up properly.'

'You sound like a wife,' he murmured, laughing gently, and she tossed him a wry look, tempering it by wrinkling her nose at him.

'I seem to be yours, for better or worse.'

'And I am little better than a monsterish brute—so it must be for worse, hmm?'

Sally couldn't answer him, at least not right then, for a lump had risen in her throat. Seeing him with the two little boys had revealed a side of him she had hitherto not known, and it unsettled her equilibrium more than she wanted to admit. 'At times you're a complete enigma,' she ventured slowly as she hung the last shirt into the wardrobe. 'I'd like to change. Will you—turn your back—please?'

His soft laugh was one of genuine amusement, and his eyes lit with a devilish gleam. 'I am familiar with every inch of you, *piccina*. Why pretend otherwise?'

A delicate pink tinged her cheeks as she turned away, and she began unpacking her suitcase with determined dedication. He seemed to delight in baiting her, and it simply wasn't fair!

'I shall freshen up in the bathroom,' Luke drawled from across the room. 'You have above five minutes before I return.'

Sally glanced round and saw that he had already changed his suit for casual trousers and a shirt left unbuttoned at the neck. She nodded, not deigning to speak, and as soon as the door closed behind him she stripped down to her underwear, then donned a floral-patterned skirt and a loose muslin top. Her hair needed a quick brush, her lips a touch of colour, and she was ready when Luke re-entered the room.

Together they walked towards the lounge in the front of the house, and as they entered the boys scrambled over each other to reach Luke, who laughingly scooped them up into his arms.

Angelina was openly friendly, and Sally found no difficulty in reciprocating. Her offer to help in the kitchen and with the children was accepted, and although they were slightly cautious, the boys soon forgot their shyness and included her in their conversation.

Lunch was a lighthearted affair, and it was while Sally and Angelina were attending to the dishes that she learnt something which surprised her somewhat.

'Does Luke always spend Christmas with you?' Sally asked idly as she applied the tea-towel to several plates, and Angelina gave her a quick smile.

'We spend it together—not always here. Sometimes Frank and I take the children down to Sydney. Have you known my brother for very long?'

The question was one of genuine curiosity, and Sally gave her answer careful thought. 'About three weeks—give or take a few days. It—it was pretty much a whirlwind courtship.'

Angelina laughed, then cast Sally a wicked grin. 'Luke always did have the knack of making split-second decisions. And knowing him as I do, he would not have given you any chance to change your mind.'

Sally swallowed convulsively and managed a sheepish smile. 'No, not really.'

'You must have both been instantly attracted to one another,' the other girl declared, and Sally made a monosyllabic reply.

This was fast becoming an inquisition of which she wanted little part, and with what she hoped was an adroit change of subject she switched the topic of conversation towards cooking, querying various Italian-style recipes and the assorted herbs and spices used. By the time they'd exhausted that subject the dishes had been disposed of.

However, later that afternoon when both girls were once again in the kitchen, this time to prepare dinner, Sally was given a subtle explanation regarding Luke's association with various women. It was almost as if Angelina wanted to discount them as being of no consequence, Sally thought ruefully, endeavouring to look the radiant newly-married wife who was confident of a mutual love to which no harm could possibly come.

With what she hoped was an understanding shrug, Sally ventured, 'I was aware that Luke had a rakish reputation. He's a very attractive man, and it would be stupid to expect him to have led a blameless existence.'

'He has had his choice of many women, but I doubt he has given a tinker's cuss for any one of them.' Angelina looked suddenly anxious. 'You do love him? I could not bear it if you married him solely for his money.'

Oh dear God! How much worse could this get? Carefully Sally said with considerable constraint, 'I didn't marry Luke for any material gain.'

'I am so glad.'

Angelina looked as if she was about to weep with relief, Sally decided wryly, wondering how she was going to stay the distance for eight days. It made her seek Luke's company with undisguised pleasure—so much so that he raised a quizzical eyebrow and bent his head down low to hers.

'*Cara*, you are very convincing—almost too convincing,' he mocked softly, and Sally gazed at him with as much fondness as she could muster. Anyone looking at them could be forgiven for thinking they were murmuring sweet nothings to each other.

'Darling Luke—the Spanish Inquisition has nothing on Angelina! I'm beginning to run out of evasive replies.'

His eyes gleamed darkly as he smiled, and his face was so close she could feel his breath stir the hair at her temples.

'I am the only family she has,' he explained. 'Consequently her concern is understandable.'

'If this goes on for much longer, I shall need rescuing,' she advised sweetly. 'It might be as well if you do some reassuring of your own.' The words were scarcely out of her mouth before he moved fractionally closer and bestowed a gentle lingering kiss on her parted lips. It shook her composure and tore it to shreds. There was a poignancy about his action she found difficult to assimilate, and his tenderness was almost her undoing. Shakily, she whispered, 'That wasn't quite fair.'

'But all is fair in love and war, is it not, *piccina*?' Luke mocked gently. 'Besides, you asked for reassurance.'

'I didn't mean a public display of affection,' she murmured fiercely, and was mortified by the devilish gleam that lit his dark eyes. Oh, he was the absolute limit!

Dinner that evening was strictly an informal affair,

and later when the children were all asleep and secure for the night there was much laughter as gaily-wrapped gifts were hung on the Christmas tree, and those too big or too heavy were placed on the floor.

It was very late when they retired to bed, having sat sipping wine for some time out on the screened verandah in search of the cooler evening air. Six hundred-odd miles further north of Sydney, Brisbane enjoyed a measurably warmer climate that was particularly noticeable in the height of summer.

As soon as the bedroom door was closed Sally turned to regard Luke warily, unsure of his intention from the mockery evident in his gaze.

'Unless you have any objection I'll take the bed nearest the window,' she stated, swivelling her eyes away as he began unbuttoning his shirt. He didn't answer, and she shed her top and quickly unfastened the clasp of her bra in an effort to don a nightgown before he had the opportunity to watch her actions, for despite two and a half weeks of shared intimacies she was painfully shy of disrobing in his presence.

As soon as she had slid the nightgown over her head she turned to face him. 'If I plead tiredness and a—headache,' she began tentatively, 'would you——'

'Leave you alone?' One eyebrow arched as he surveyed her. 'Why, *piccina*, do you have a headache?'

'Would you believe me if I say yes?'

'Come here.' It was a softly-voiced command, but nonetheless there was hidden steel beneath the surface, and she crossed to stand in front of him, one hand sliding down the length of her hair in a defensive gesture.

Luke's hand reached out to tuck a stray lock of hair behind her ear, then he sought her chin and lifted it. For timeless seconds he subjected her to an unwavering scrutiny, then the edges of his mouth lifted into a slight smile. 'For all that you think you hate me, I am not totally insensitive. Choose your bed, *cara*. You have your wish to sleep alone.' He bent his head and touched his lips to her forehead.

Sally fought against the desire to wind her arms up around his neck as his gentleness touched a chord deep inside, and rather shakily she stepped back, turning away from him as she slid back the covers on the bed nearest her.

As soon as her head touched the pillow Luke switched off the light, and she waited with bated breath for him to occupy the other bed, consciously counting the seconds until she heard the rustle of linen and the slight sound of his weight depressing the mattress.

Sally awoke to the sound of excited children's voices, and she lifted a hand to glimpse the time from her wristwatch. Six o'clock! She rolled over and caught sight of Luke standing near the end of the bed tucking his shirt into his trousers.

'Good morning—Merry Christmas,' she greeted him with a slight smile. Today was not for arguments. It was Christmas, and there were presents and children, and the joy of watching gifts being unwrapped and exclaimed over; huge quantities of food to be eaten, wine to be drunk, and overall it was a time of peace and goodwill.

'*Buon Natale, cara*,' Luke answered gently. 'You slept well, eh? The headache is gone?'

'Yes—oh, listen to them!' she grinned widely, and couldn't help the laugh that bubbled to the surface. 'I think they're trying to guess what's in all the presents.'

'To be sure. Can you not remember the time when

you did the same?'

'Is it too early for us to go out yet?'

Luke began to chuckle. 'I imagine Angelina is having quite a time trying to keep their noise to a minimum. She will be relieved when we make our appearance.'

'When are the children allowed to open their presents?' she queried, slipping out of bed. Quickly she donned her robe.

'Ah, your childhood is not so far behind you, hmm?' Luke mocked gently, coming to stand in front of her. 'First, we all have breakfast together, then we go to church. After we return home, it is then time for the presents.'

A little startled, she said slowly, 'I'm not of your faith——'

'It matters little, Sally,' he answered gravely. 'I doubt He will mind from which house of worship you choose to celebrate the day of His birth.'

After they had breakfasted, they all slid into the station-wagon and Frank drove the short distance to church. Sally held Gianni on her lap while Luke balanced Luigi on one knee, and little Lisa snuggled close to Angelina on the front seat.

Their return home brought whoops of excitement from both boys, who tore from the station-wagon to the front porch where they hopped impatiently from one foot to the other waiting for their father to unlock the door.

Sally felt herself carried along with the fun of it all, and she helped the boys sort out the presents. It was almost like being a child all over again watching the children unwrap their gifts, and it was a sight not to be forgotten to witness their laughter and their joy.

There were three presents for her—an opal bracelet

from Angelina and Frank, a box of toiletries from the children, and Luke's gift brought forth a gasp of admiration, for it was a gold medallion depicting the Madonna and Child on a delicate chain of gold.

Genuine tears shone in her eyes as she thanked them all, the boys giggling with delight as she hugged them, then Angelina and Frank, until she came to Luke. Without any pretence she reached up on tiptoe and kissed him.

Luke received a beautiful oil painting depicting an ocean liner on the high seas in the height of a storm which Angelina had taken several months to paint in her spare time.

'Something for you to remember of our voyage from Italy, *mio fratello*,' Angelina murmured gently, and Sally could tell that he was touched by the gesture, for his expression assumed incredible gentleness as he looked across at his sister.

Sally's choice of gift for Luke had been difficult, for what could you buy for a man who appeared to have everything? In the end she had chosen an expensive cigarette lighter, and a large box of his favourite cheroots.

The main meal of the day was to be eaten at one o'clock, and Sally left Luke and Frank to entertain the boys with all their presents while she helped Angelina in the kitchen. Little Lisa was fractious with her first tooth, and she was passed from her mother to Sally in an effort to keep her happy, until at midday she was fed, changed and put down for her afternoon nap.

Angelina had excelled herself in the kitchen, for there was a starter of prawns in a nest of lettuce, roast turkey that melted in the mouth, sliced ham and chicken, and rice salad as well as coleslaw, beetroot and tomatoes. Dessert was a lemon ice, *gelato*, and to finish a slice of delicious cake. They all donned paper hats, pulled Christmas crackers with hilarious results, and drank champagne.

By the time the table was cleared and the dishes dealt with it was mid-afternoon, and they sought the relative coolness of the screened verandah to sit on cane chairs and relax with a cool drink. The boys, tired from rising so early that morning, collapsed and were lifted on to their beds for a nap.

In the evening, after a late meal of cold meats and a salad, they took the children for a swim in the pool, then after a shower the three little tots were settled down for the night.

The following day set a precedent for the days that followed. Sally and Luke both rose early to swim in the pool, then they showered and dressed in time for breakfast, after which together with Angelina, Frank and the children, they would set off for the day with a picnic lunch, returning late in the afternoon. The evenings after the children retired to bed were spent on the screened verandah, where with a cool drink in hand they talked far into the night. It was then that Sally learnt much about Luke and Angelina as children in post-war Italy, the hardships they had been forced to face, and the struggle to exist without parents or any close relatives on which to call. She saw with sudden clarity the youth Luke had been so many years before, burdened with responsibility and an irrepressible desire to ascend beyond poverty. She glimpsed a young man denied the joys of carefree living, the fun times, the laughter—until all too recently. And now his sweat-acquired wealth had failed to buy what he needed above all—a woman to love him.

There were no parties or social occasions during

their stay, for Angelina confided to Sally that Luke preferred it this way.

'For much of the year we do not see one another,' she imparted, shrugging a little. 'When we do, we wish to spend the time in each other's company. There is plenty of time for friends.'

The children were a delight, and Sally found herself viewing each passing day with a tinge of regret, for it meant one day closer to her return to Sydney where once again she and Luke would undoubtedly resort to their former state of antipathy. As improbable as it seemed, they had scarcely exchanged a cross word while under Angelina's roof, and even the nights were magical as Luke's lovemaking took on a sensual, gently seducing quality that melted her resistance and made a traitor of her treacherous emotions. Long after she lay in his sleeping arms she would blush at the depth of feeling he was able to arouse, and the soul-searching she subjected herself to did little to resolve the many 'ifs', for it seemed none of them were likely to come to any account.

On the day of their return, barely an hour before they were due to drive to Brisbane, Angelina took Sally aside, and her face betrayed a mixture of earnest concern.

'Look after my brother well—he needs someone like you, gentle and loving, with the ability to make him laugh.' She smiled, then gave Sally an affectionate hug. 'Love him as he deserves to be loved, I beg of you.'

Sally gave a strangled reply, although exactly what she couldn't recall, and it was perhaps fortunate that Lisa awoke crying from her morning nap at that precise moment.

The children came to the airport, and were surprisingly good during the drive from Surfers' Paradise to Brisbane, and their farewells were a trifle tearful as Sally followed Luke out from the departure lounge and on to the tarmac.

It had been a wonderful holiday, and one she looked forward to repeating. She waved until the plane taxied out of sight, and as it sped down the runway and lifted to ascend high above the clouds she hastily selected a magazine and buried her nose in the printed pages to hide the prick of tears that stung her eyes.

Sally didn't offer so much as a word during the short flight to Sydney, except for a monosyllabic acceptance or refusal of the refreshments offered by a hovering hostess. It was something of a relief when the jet landed at Kingsford-Smith airport, and she stood in reflective silence as Luke waited to collect their luggage. He refused her offer to carry one of the suitcases, and she walked at his side through the terminal building to the pavement outside where she was instructed to wait beside the luggage while he went to collect the car.

While he was gone, she stood gazing silently into space as she thought of the house in Vaucluse that was now her home, of Carlo, and lastly of her father. It could be so different, if only——

Luke brought the Alfa-Romeo to a smooth halt beside the kerb, and with a slight sigh Sally moved forward to open the passenger door. Once inside, she closed the door with a decisive click, watching from veiled lashes as he slid out from behind the wheel. She was aware that he stowed their suitcases into the boot, and she contrived a smile as he slipped back behind the wheel.

'What is occupying your thoughts?' Luke queried musingly as he set the car in motion, swinging it into the heavy flow of traffic vacating the airport. 'You have a particularly pensive air—in fact, during the entire flight you said scarcely a word.'

'We carried it off fairly well, didn't we?' Sally countered reflectively, and a hand lifted to smooth back a stray lock of hair behind one ear.

'I am positive my sister thinks we have an idyllic marriage,' he drawled, and his voice held an edge of mockery that stirred an all too familiar resentment.

'We, of course, know different.'

'Do not harbour any devious schemes now that we are home, *piccina*.'

At that slightly ruthless injunction she burst into angry speech, turning to face him with eyes that sparked with utter fury. 'What schemes could I devise? I'm irrevocably chained to you for as long as you choose. Even if I were to contemplate leaving you, the thought that you'd remove your financial backing from my father's business is a sufficient deterrent. The price is a son,' she choked, then looked away from him, for suddenly the sight of that harsh profile was too much to bear. 'Poor child,' she went on to mutter fervently. 'Its birth will probably be as hellish as its conception!'

'*Dio potente!*'

At his savage imprecation she rushed on heedlessly, 'What chance will it have with parents who hate each other? That's no way to raise children—they need love, and security——'

'That is enough! *Cristo*, must I be berated in the midst of negotiating city traffic?'

She subsided into angry silence, staring straight ahead for the remainder of the drive to Vaucluse, and the instant the car came to a halt in the garage she made to slide out, only to have her wrist caught in a bone-crushing grip.

'Oh no,' Luke declared with ominous softness. 'Before you escape into the house you will answer me one question.' His eyes gleamed with cold anger, and she felt a shiver of fear feather the length of her spine. 'What makes you think our children will be deprived of love—yours, mine?' The silky query was none the less dangerous for being quietly voiced, and she ran her tongue along her lips in a nervous gesture.

'Their lives will hardly be auspicious—we're always fighting,' she flung shakily, and he gave a sardonic smile.

'Can you not conceive of a time when we might not fight?'

His evasive response set her mind reeling, and blindly she slid out from the car and ran to the entrance foyer as if countless demons were in pursuit. At the top of the first flight of stairs she came to an abrupt halt.

'Mother!' Her voice came out as a barely audible squeak, and she uttered in shocked disbelief, 'Emily —what are you doing here?'

One eyebrow rose in faint humour. 'My dear daughter, I did declare my intention to come, and here I am. Why sound so surprised?' Elegantly dressed, her hair stylishly coiffured, Emily bore little resemblance to her daughter.

Sally gathered her scattered wits together, completely unaware that Luke had ascended the stairs and was now standing behind her. 'I mean, how did you get in? We've been away—so has Carlo,' she explained hastily as Emily gave an expansive smile.

'Dearest Sally!' Emily spread her arms in welcome, and Sally moved forward to receive the maternal embrace. 'A call to your father revealed the expected date of your return, and I arranged my arrival accordingly.

Your father met me at the airport, where he very graciously bought me lunch, then he deposited me here only two hours ago. I've unpacked my things into one of the guest rooms your manservant allotted me. Now,' she allowed her features to crease in a conciliatory smile as her gaze went beyond Sally's shoulder, 'let me meet my son-in-law.'

Sally stood in dazed silence as Luke moved forward, and she felt his arm settle about her waist as he took Emily's hand in a firm grip.

'You may call me Emily,' that good lady declared condescendingly. 'I am "Mother" only to my daughter, and even then I much prefer her to address me by name.' She looked up at him with a searching appraisal that would have daunted a lesser man. 'You look incredibly Italian, and as you're so tall, I venture to conclude you come from one of the northern provinces. Wealthy, undoubtedly,' she paused and moved a fluid hand to encompass the house and its furnishings. 'All this is scarcely the trappings of a poor man.'

'Shall we move into the lounge?' Luke suggested smoothly. 'Perhaps you would welcome a glass of sherry, Emily? If not, there is an ample selection of wines and spirits from which to choose.' His arm stayed firmly about Sally's waist as he propelled her forward.

'Bourbon with ice, no water,' Emily intimated, adding a charming, 'Thank you, Luke.'

'Sally, a sherry, or something stronger?'

Sally caught the glint of wry humour in his eyes, and directing him a stunning smile she said lightly, 'Sherry will be fine, thank you, darling.' Turning to her mother, she asked, 'Did you have a smooth flight over?'

'Of course,' Emily replied, and Sally hid a smile.

Faced with Emily's singlemindedness she doubted either the Boeing jet or the elements would dare to create so much as a ripple of discord.

'How long do you expect to stay?'

Emily cast her daughter a direct look. 'With you, darling? Precisely eight days, altogether—five now, then I shall fly to Perth for a week, after which I will go on to Darwin for approximately the same length of time. The remaining three days before returning to New York I intend spending with you.'

'How is Hank?' Sally queried with interest of her mother's second husband, who was a nice man, tall, bluff and typically American.

'Well. Busy, of course,' Emily conceded. 'The wheels of big business can be time-consuming. What do you do?' she queried suddenly of Luke.

'I am a business consultant and financier,' Luke answered with a scarcely detectable drawl, and Emily cast him a speculative look.

'A very successful one, I gather.'

Luke inclined his head, and Sally elected to make her escape.

'Darling, you talk to Mother while I check with Carlo what we're having for dinner.' The glance she cast him was as loving as she could make it, but there was an angry gleam in the depths of her eyes that was met and matched by an answering glint in the dark eyes not too far from her own.

In the kitchen she greeted Carlo with a wide smile, and sniffed appreciatively. 'Mmm, that smells delicious. Is there anything I can do to help?'

Carlo shook his head. 'You are looking well. You enjoyed your holiday?'

'It was very relaxing,' she answered carefully. 'The children were a bundle of fun. Which room did you put my mother in?'

'The one nearest the stairs,' he informed her. 'She is a little——'

'Overpowering?' Sally laughed. 'She takes a bit of getting used to. The trick is not to let her daunt you. Shall I set the table?'

'If you wish,' Carlo agreed with a slight nod. 'However, I can do it if you want to join Luke and your mother.'

'Shh!' Sally murmured humorously. 'Besides, my being here will give Luke and Emily a chance to get acquainted.'

It was ten minutes before she threw Carlo an impish wave and departed back down the hallway to the lounge.

'Dinner will be ready in five minutes,' she told them as she crossed the room to join them.

Emily looked up and smiled serenely. 'Luke has been filling me in with the details of how you met each other.'

Sally swallowed convulsively. 'Oh,' she managed a trifle hesitantly. 'That would have been interesting.'

'We must go out shopping during the next few days,' her mother declared. 'Luke tells me he'll be away, so you and I will have plenty of time to ourselves to chat and catch up with all the news.'

Oh dear, Sally groaned, for that meant that what information Emily was unable to inveigle Luke into divulging about himself, Emily intended winkling it out of her daughter. The next few days would be 'question-time' with a vengeance!

Aloud, she said brightly, 'Shall we go in to dinner?'

The veal Carlo had prepared was superb, but Sally didn't register tasting it as she forked a few pieces into her mouth, and afterwards she had no idea what the

salad greens comprised, or for that matter, what she
ate for dessert. She was only aware of Luke's forceful
presence directly opposite, and Emily's all too discern-
ing appraisal and that good lady's voiced inquisitive-
ness. It was an extreme relief when the meal ended,
and coffee was taken in the lounge. At least there she
could move around, and was not confined to the table
without any legitimate form of escape.

Luke, to give him credit, was at his most urbane,
and Sally marvelled that he could appear so calm when
beneath that rugged exterior smouldered an anger of
which only she was aware. Her own sparkling façade
seemed to develop a crack or two, which she fervently
hoped escaped Emily's notice.

At nine-thirty Luke made the apologetic excuse of
paperwork requiring his attention, and with a prof-
fered handshake to his mother-in-law, a brief touch
of his lips to Sally's temple, he departed for the study.

Almost as soon as the door closed behind him, Emily
moved from her chair to occupy the empty space beside
Sally on the settee.

'Your husband is a most charming man,' she complimented tolerantly, her eyebrows creasing slightly as
she chose her words. 'Certainly he possesses—oh,
what's the word I want? Charisma, that's it. Yes,' she
nodded slightly, fixing her daughter with a roguish
smile, 'I imagine he's good in bed——'

'Mother!'

Emily spread her hands eloquently. 'My dear, why
hide one's head in the sand? Shared intimacies are an
integral part of married life. While not all-important,
it's certainly more agreeable if one adores rather than
abhors what goes on in the bedroom.' Her eyes
swivelled speculatively to Sally's hands, and reaching
out she touched her daughter's rings. 'None of these

are inexpensive, and that wristwatch must be worth a packet. He treats you well, doesn't he?'

How could Sally deny it? 'Luke is very generous, Emily. I'm very happy.'

'Are you?' her mother queried critically. 'Certainly you endeavour to give that impression, but beneath it all—I wonder,' she concluded thoughtfully, and Sally summoned up every ounce of acting ability, and she even managed a laugh as she sought to reassure.

'Oh, Emily, you are an impossible sceptic! Luke is —one of the most sophisticated, cynical men I've ever met.' She smiled impishly—if awards were being given out, she undoubtedly deserved one! 'Every time I look at him, I marvel that he chose someone as ordinary as me. Probably in a year or so I'll be quite blasée about the whole thing, but after only about three weeks of marriage I'm still in a state of awe.'

'Hmm, I'll accept that.'

Sally gave an inaudible sigh of relief that was short-lived as her mother queried with devastating directness, 'Just what is it your father is being evasive about? His hearty reply to my query regarding his health brought forth an immediate avowal that he'd never felt better. While I, not having seen him for some years, couldn't help noticing more visible careworn signs than I expected. Is he ill?'

Oh lord, this was getting worse instead of better! Carefully Sally met Emily's alert gaze, and couldn't resist teasing lightly, 'Why, Mother, I do believe you have a soft spot for Daddy, after all.'

'I like your father, Sally. For a few years I even believed myself to be in love with him. Unfortunately, it proved to be a delusion. However, that doesn't prevent me from expressing concern for his welfare.'

Sally tried to gloss over the facts, assuring her, 'He's

had a few business worries—nothing catastrophic,' she hastened. 'But he's had a few anxious moments that have taken their toll. He's under a doctor's care, and there's no cause for alarm.'

'I believe what you're telling me—it's what you're not saying that worries me!'

'Why not ask Joe himself? He'll tell you exactly the same.'

Emily brightened somewhat, and shifting comfortably, she settled back against the cushions. 'You must telephone him tomorrow and arrange lunch. It will be like old times'—she laughed deprecatorily—'well, not quite. You were only a child. But it would be nice for the three of us to have lunch together. Now, my dear, I'll avail myself of a nightcap, then go to my room. At my age, travelling gets to be tiring. A small brandy, perhaps?'

'Of course,' Sally responded lightly. 'I'll get it for you.'

'Thank you, darling. I shan't rise early in the morning, but if you could see that I have some coffee sent up around eight-thirty?' Emily smiled a trifle wickedly. 'You can then bid your husband a fond farewell without me hovering discreetly in the background.'

Sally waited a few minutes after her mother left the lounge before following her example. Luke appeared to be ensconced in the study for some time, and in any case, it would be infinitely wiser if she were already in bed and asleep when he came upstairs. She wasn't in the mood for recriminations, and besides, she felt rather weary.

Within ten minutes she had showered and slipped between the sheets to lie in the dark in wakeful silence for what seemed an age before sleep finally beckoned, and then she seemed only to have closed her eyes when a slight sound alerted her to Luke's presence.

Quite desperately she wanted him to reach out and gather her close—if nothing else, she needed the reassurance of his need of her, for then she could lose herself in his passion and drift through an euphoric haze where emotions overruled reality.

There were silent tears that slid ignominiously down her cheeks long after Luke, without making any touching contact whatever, lapsed into deep and uncontrived slumber, and in the morning she woke to find the bed empty, learning from Carlo as soon as she entered the kitchen that Luke had caught the early flight to Adelaide.

CHAPTER NINE

'WELL, darling, what shall we do today?'

Sally looked across the breakfast table and shook her head negatively. 'Whatever you want—I don't mind.'

It was two days after Luke's departure, and she had become increasingly distracted, unable to fasten her attention on anything for very long. Yesterday they had spent the day shopping, wandering at leisure among the many arcades in the inner city, and Emily had expressed a desire to repeat the exercise. Somehow the thought of wandering the city streets aimlessly in search of the best bargain in clothing had lost its appeal, but anything was better than staying home where everything reminded her so vividly of Luke.

'Dear girl, you look positively forlorn,' Emily chided with a maternal cluck of her tongue. 'Ring your father —we'll meet him for lunch. Tell him somewhere expensive, and it's to be my treat. The cure for the blues, my dear, is a shopping spree.' She arched one eyebrow in deliberate query. 'I imagine Luke can well afford to pamper you with one? Now, hurry and finish your coffee, and we'll not waste time.'

And waste time they did not! Sally's head positively reeled as Emily led her from one shop to the other, adding parcels and packages of all sizes and description, so that she became rather fatalistic over the number of cheques she was signing. The back seat of the car became laden, and heaven knew what she was going to do with so many new clothes. It was commendable to possess a wide and varied wardrobe—

but not to acquire it in so short a time!

True to her word, Emily chose one of the better restaurants, and they had been seated for no more than five minutes when Joe arrived. They chose to order an aperitif while perusing the menu, and Sally, who had no appetite at all, ordered soup, declined the main course, and decided on dessert. Joe teased her unmercifully, declaring the reason to be Luke's absence, and hinting at a more pertinent cause which Sally immediately disclaimed, even though a tiny seed of doubt worried otherwise.

'Well, well—a family luncheon, no less, with one member conspicuously absent.'

Sally looked up and met Chantrelle's glittery eyes, and felt her heart lurch. It seemed the other girl was dogging her footsteps, whether accidentally or on purpose she couldn't decide.

'Luke is in Adelaide on business,' she replied evenly, then aware that introductions were necessary she performed them with as much aplomb as she could manage. 'Chantrelle Bakersfield—my mother, Emily Breckenridge-Browning.'

'Good heavens,' Chantrelle said faintly. 'I thought Sally's mother lived in exile in America.'

'I live in New York,' Emily explained to her sweetly, 'but hardly in exile.'

'Are you consoling Sally while her husband is away? Oh, Sally!' Chantrelle turned and shot her a vicious smile. 'You know, of course, that Carmela went along for the ride? But then Luke would have told you, I'm sure.'

'Why shouldn't Carmela be in Adelaide, Chantrelle?' Sally asked quietly. 'She's an accountant, and she works closely with Luke.'

'Close?' The other girl laughed derisively. 'That's

an understatement!'

Emily directed Chantrelle a levelling glance. 'We are in the middle of what was an enjoyable meal. I'm sure you've said whatever it is you want to say. Goodbye, Miss—er——' she deliberately let her voice trip vaguely over the name, then returned her attention to the contents of the plate in front of her, thereby disclaiming any further interest.

'Goodbye, Chantrelle,' Sally murmured. 'I can't say it's been a pleasure, but then,' she added with seeming winsomeness, 'you aren't a very pleasant person, are you?'

Chantrelle swung her chin up sulkily, then waltzed off to sit several tables away near the rear of the restaurant.

'I think,' Joe began with quiet anger, 'that girl is the most objectionable young woman I've ever met. How two people as charming as Charles and Andrea managed to end up with someone like Chantrelle for a daughter is beyond me.'

'She's a troublemaker,' Emily discerned blandly. 'And troublemakers have a habit of destroying themselves, given time. Now, I refuse to waste any more time even talking about that awful girl.'

It was all very well to dismiss it so lightly, but Sally relived the scene over and over again through the rest of the day, her mind constantly in a turmoil at the vision Chantrelle's words aroused. Luke hadn't mentioned Carmela accompanying him, but then he hadn't really had the opportunity, and perhaps he would have if they hadn't argued and been confronted with Emily on their doorstep. It was that little green monster again, she cursed roundly.

That night Sally slept badly to wake feeling as if she hadn't closed her eyes at all.

'You look dreadful.'

Sally viewed her mother over the breakfast table and offered a wry grimace by way of reply.

'What you need is a day of pampering,' Emily determined firmly. 'We'll go into the city and spend several hours at a beauty salon. Hair, facial, manicure —the entire thing! Then we'll go on to dinner, and even take in a movie. Yes?'

'Why not?'

They did, after instructing Carlo to take the day and the evening off, and for the first time in her life Sally submitted to the ministrations offered by one of Sydney's exclusive salons.

Her hair was fractionally trimmed and shampooed, then rolled into fat spongy rollers which looked incongruous when she caught sight of her reflection in the mirror. After partial drying beneath the drier, the rollers were covered with a towel while another girl gave her a facial. Then there was the application of make-up, after which a pretty young teenager attended to the manicuring of Sally's nails. Her hair was then styled with a blow-dryer and given a light film of hairspray to hold it in place.

The result was quite breathtaking, and Sally walked out of the salon feeling elegant and the epitome of sophistication. The expense was breathtaking as well, but the twinge of conscience was only momentary!

'You look ravishing, my dear,' Emily complimented. 'It's lamentable that Luke isn't here to see you.'

'You look rather gorgeous yourself,' Sally smiled easily.

'Now that the exchange of mutual admiration has been dealt with,' her mother declared, 'let's decide what we shall do next. It's much too early to contemplate dinner, but we could drive home and change into something more glamorous. Something to match our new look? We could have a drink, then book a table somewhere, and as yet we haven't decided which movie we should see.'

'Lead on, Mother,' Sally directed impishly. 'You seem to be in command. I'll just follow wherever you lead.'

They had scarcely been in the house thirty minutes when the telephone rang, and Sally crossed to the nearest extension.

'Hello—who is speaking?'

'None other than your husband, *cara*,' a rather droll voice answered.

'Luke?' she queried in disbelief, then contrived to make her voice sound welcoming. 'Is that really you, darling?'

'Did you not expect me to call you at least once during my absence?' His voice was a cynical drawl as he continued, 'I gather from your effusive greeting that Emily is within hearing distance.'

'Yes,' Sally answered cautiously. 'How is everything going?' Taking courage from the distance separating them, she added with contrived seductiveness, 'You don't need to ask how much I miss you.'

Luke's throaty chuckle sounded along the wire, and conscious of her mother's interested gaze she forced her features to assume a dreamy wistful expression.

'My darling wife, I could almost be persuaded to disregard business and catch the next flight home.'

'Oh, you mustn't do that,' she hastened quickly. 'Besides, Emily and I are having a wonderful time. We've been shopping almost every day.' She couldn't resist adding sweetly, 'I hope everything is going to your satisfaction. I've no doubt having Carmela there is a great help. I ran into Chantrelle yesterday, and she took great delight in passing on that piece of information.'

'Thank the good *Dio* for the distance between us, *mia sposa*,' Luke threatened softly. 'Otherwise I would shake you until you begged for mercy.'

'You say the nicest things, Luke,' she murmured. 'When are you coming home?'

'Unfortunately, not until Tuesday. I will let you know which flight. *Ciao, piccina*.' With those mocking words he replaced the receiver, and after a few seconds Sally did likewise.

'That was Luke, of course.'

Sally looked across the room and met her mother's interested gaze. 'Yes. He's been delayed a few days. He won't be home until after the weekend.'

'What a shame,' Emily declared. 'I was looking forward to spending more time with him. Now it will have to wait until I return from Darwin.'

Sally moved towards the drinks cabinet, busying her hands in an effort to remain calm. The sound of Luke's voice had started up the familar ache in her heart, and she was vexed beyond measure that he should possess the power to stir her emotions so ridiculously.

'Sherry, Mother?' she queried out loud, and rather absently poured vermouth instead.

'Dear child, you aren't concentrating at all, are you?'

'I'm sorry,' Sally declared blankly. 'What did you say?'

With great fortitude Emily collected her glass and crossed to Sally's side, adding lemonade, ice and a slice of lemon. 'You love him very much, don't you?'

'I——' Sally swallowed the lump in her throat, then nodded slowly. 'Yes—yes, I do.' There, she'd admitted it at last.

'I'm very pleased. You've made a good marriage, I

can see that for myself.'

Good—pleased? Sally felt hysterical laughter rise up inside her, and stifled it with considerable effort.

'I'm sorry for doubting your judgment,' Emily continued gently. 'I was so afraid you'd made some ghastly mistake you might repent later. However, I can now leave with an untroubled conscience.' She beamed across at Sally, and gave a brilliant smile. 'You'll both have to visit us in New York. Hank would be delighted.'

'Thank you, Emily.' In a minute she'd give herself away! 'Shall we finish our drinks, then make our way to the restaurant? And as yet, we haven't decided which movie to see.'

It was very late when they arrived back home that night, and Sally crept into bed feeling pleasantly tired. It had been a very enjoyable day, and now the weekend stretched interminably ahead of her. Quite how she would manage to get through four more days without Luke didn't bear thinking about. The sound of his voice on the telephone had reawakened the treacherous desire she tried so hard to curb, and his beloved face haunted her dreams so that awake or asleep she was never free of his image.

On Saturday morning they toured the museum, and after a light lunch, Emily declared an interest in inspecting the Opera House. She was quite dauntless, Sally mused affectionately as they came out into the direct heat of the sun and stood admiring the sparkling warm waters of the harbour.

'Joe shall take us to dinner tonight.'

At such certainty in her mother's voice, Sally began to protest. 'He may have plans of his own, and besides, it's too short notice.'

'Nonsense,' Emily determined briskly. 'We'll drive to his apartment now—a much better idea than ringing him.'

What chance did she have? Sally thought quizzically —or for that matter, Joe?

On reflection, it was an extremely enjoyable evening, for they frequented a small Italian restaurant run entirely by one family, and the food was excellent. The atmosphere proved authentic, with musical entertainment being provided by the singing of traditional songs to the accompaniment of a piano accordion.

The following day they rose early and packed a picnic lunch, electing to visit the Botanical Gardens, then go on to Bondi Beach for the remainder of the day.

Early on Monday morning Sally drove Emily to the airport, and after seeing her safely on to the plane en route to Perth, she drove into the city.

Parking the car, she made her way along the familiar lane to 'Claude's', entering the kitchen to glimpse the hive of activity usually projected by those who worked within.

'Sally! *Mon dieu!*' Claude exclaimed with surprise. 'What are you doing here?'

'Am I not welcome?' she couldn't resist teasing, and saw his smile.

'Of course, of course. It is just that I did not expect to see you,' he reassured. 'All is well?' He skinned several onions and chopped them with deft precision. 'You are perhaps shopping?'

'Yes and no,' she laughed. 'I've just seen my mother off at the airport, my husband is away, and I have several hours on my hands with very little to do. I thought I'd call in and see a few friends. Do you mind?'

'If you stay here for very long I shall forget you

no longer work for me, and enlist your talents.'

'Someone is away?' she queried idly, and he nodded. 'I'll stay for a few hours—the whole day, if you need me,' she added with sudden inspiration. It was just what she needed to occupy the empty hours and keep her from constantly thinking of Luke. There was nothing at home that she could do, apart from cooking, and as it was Carlo's evening off it seemed ridiculous to prepare a three-course meal for just one person.

It was well after eleven o'clock that night before she fell into bed, feeling pleasantly tired after the first hard day's work she had completed since marrying Luke, and she slept soundly until the alarm clock roused her at eight the following morning.

Today Luke was coming home. Already her stomach was behaving peculiarly, with butterfly wings beating a nervous tattoo, and she hadn't had breakfast yet. What would she be like by this afternoon?

Even Carlo noticed her lack of appetite, and commented on it as he removed plates whose contents had hardly been touched.

'There is something else you would prefer?'

Sally cast him an apologetic smile. 'No, thank you. I'm just not hungry. Do you—do you know what time Luke is expected home?' Ridiculous—if she didn't know, how would Carlo be expected to know?

'He invariably rings from the airport on arrival. I imagine he will be home for dinner. Do you wish to prepare it?'

'Would you mind? It will keep me busy.'

Carlo gave her an understanding grin. 'And that is all-important, is it not?'

'Yes.' Her mind flew over the menu—something special, with candles and wine, and afterwards—Oh God, why did she have to fall in love with him? He hadn't professed any love for her—what was more, he wasn't likely to! She was just an instrument by which he could beget a much-wanted son. There were times when she almost thought he cared, but passion and love were not the same and she was too inexperienced to tell the difference.

How she managed to get through the remainder of the day was a small miracle, for each hour seemed to drag by with impossible slowness.

At eight o'clock Sally served dinner for herself and Carlo, declining to use the dining-room and an elaborate setting. The kitchen was more friendly, and after the dishes had been cleared away and dealt with, she wandered into the *salotto* with the intention of watching television.

At ten she crossed to the drinks cabinet and poured herself a mild-tasting semi-sweet sherry. Confidence, she assured herself as she sipped the amber-coloured liquid. Twenty minutes later she refilled her glass with a deliberate sense of calm. She felt warm inside, and just the slightest bit floaty. It was a feeling she wanted to cultivate—anything was better than the tension that had been tearing her nerves to pieces for most of the day.

Luke—what was he thinking at this precise moment? Preparing to do battle with an argumentative wife, most probably, Sally thought with a faint grimace. Their relationship had been anything but smooth —except in bed. How long could she go on hating herself for loving him—because she did love him, quite shamelessly. Such a confession would surely bring a smile of amusement to his lips! There was no doubt he lusted after her—but loved? How could he, when she had assured him at every turn how much she hated him?

Oh God, where was he? An hour had passed, bringing worry and a degree of anxiety. Perhaps he wasn't
coming home at all. That was a chilling thought, and
one she dismissed almost at once. Something could
have happened, an accident——

'While you are there, pour one for me.'

Sally almost dropped her glass. She hadn't heard a
sound—although the television was on, and would have
muffled much of the noise associated with Luke's
arrival home. Slowly she turned to face him.

'You startled me!' Her eyes ran over his broad
frame, then settled with a strange sense of hunger on
his face. He looked curiously refreshed, and she
queried tentatively, 'Is it raining outside?'

Luke ran a hand over his hair, a smile tugging at
his lips. 'I had a puncture on the way home from the
airport,' he explained dryly. 'Tyre-changing at night
is not the smooth operation afforded by daylight—I
needed a shower and a change of clothes.'

Surprise showed in her expression. 'You've been
home for a while?'

'Fifteen minutes or so.' He crossed to her side and
poured himself a drink. 'More?' He held the decanter
out towards her glass, but she covered it with her hand.

His slightly raised eyebrow had her explaining, 'This
is my third.'

'Really, *cara sposa*—you need courage to greet me?'
His voice was a sardonic drawl. 'I expected you to be
in bed.'

Sally turned away, unable to face the cynicism in his
eyes. 'I was worried,' she intimated unsteadily.

'Ah, I see,' he mocked. 'You imagined an accident,
eh? No doubt you have been waiting with bated breath
for confirmation of my injuries—or worse, hmm?' His
laugh held no pretence to humour. 'Tell me, my darling

wife, would you have shed any tears over my demise?'

Sally didn't answer—she couldn't. Her voice had somehow become enmeshed in the constriction squeezing her throat, and the ache in her heart was a tangible pain. All she wanted to do was to escape from this hateful man whose subtle sarcasm had the power to hurt her unbearably.

'Lost for words?'

Sally placed her glass down on to a nearby table, then she began walking quickly towards the door.

'Sally.'

At the sound of his voice she began to run, blind panic lending wings to her feet as she fled towards the stairs.

Seconds later hands grasped hold of her shoulders, successfully bringing her to a standstill, and there was nothing she could do to escape. A tiny shiver ran the length of her body as he firmly turned her round to face him.

An imprecation that was little more than a husky murmur left his lips, and he tilted her chin, holding it fast as he gazed down at the pitiful trembling of her mouth, the blue eyes huge and drowning in tears.

After what seemed an age he leant out a hand and gently touched each of the twin rivulets trickling silently down her cheeks.

'All this——' he paused fractionally, his voice incredibly soft as a slow smile lifted his lips, 'for little more than an hour's tardiness in arriving home?'

She flung wretchedly, 'You didn't even tell me you were taking Carmela——' A hand covered her mouth, effectively silencing her.

'My sweet idiot,' he berated gently, 'I did not *take* Carmela to Adelaide. Not only did we travel on separate days, we stayed in separate hotels. Her presence was necessary for business reasons—nothing more.'

Rather shakily she attempted to brush the tears from her cheeks, but her hands were caught and held.

'*Cara?*'

'Don't call me that! I'm not your darling—I never was, and I never will be!'

'Are you not, *mia?*' he queried softly, pulling her close against him. 'You are the other half of me, *carina*, do you not know that?' His hands moved caressingly over her spine, moulding her slim body to the hardening contours of his own as his lips began a tantalising trail over her cheekbones, then he gently cradled her face. 'I love you—so very much,' he declared deeply, then a shadow of pain altered his expression. 'The torment I have endured over the unbridled display of passion I subjected you to on our wedding night— *Cristo*, to discover you were untouched!' His face paled and became incredibly bleak.

Sally wanted to cry out at the pain evident in those dark eyes, but no sound came, and she reached up to touch his cheek, her eyes widening as he caught and held her hand, pressing it to his lips.

'How you have fought me—with words, and in such a manner I would not have tolerated from anyone else! Never before has any woman had the power to make me pulsate with desire one minute, then blaze with anger the next!' He smiled down at her, teasing a little. 'There were times when I could quite cheerfully have wrung your slender neck.'

Sally declared a trifle shakily, 'You weren't exactly the required model of all the husbandly virtues.' She felt rather dazed, and unable to fully comprehend that he loved her. 'You were a rake, and an arrogant one at that! You seemed to delight in teasing me—rather like a superior cat playing with a timid mouse. It it any wonder that I retaliated?'

His eyes glowed with a deep smouldering passion, and he continued to gaze down at her upturned face with such warmth that her heart turned over and her bones seemed to melt.

'I love you.' The admission came as a shaky, tremulous whisper that he had to bend low to catch. 'Oh, Luke, I've been fighting it for so long,' she declared achingly.

'You cannot imagine how much I have wanted to hear you admit that,' he groaned gently as his lips sought the sensitive pulse at the base of her throat, then travelled slowly down to the soft curve of her breasts.

'There's something I'd like to do,' Sally began hesitantly, and he lifted his head to regard her attentively.

'Will it keep until tomorrow?' His eyes lit with wicked humour. 'I have definite plans for what remains of the night.' He chuckled softly as a vivid blush coloured her cheeks. 'Why, *cara*?' he queried tolerantly. 'What is it that you would like to do?'

Confusion lent a sparkle to her eyes, and her lips curved witchingly. 'Could we please get married?'

Luke's eyebrows arched quizzically. 'I was of the impression that we are—especially as I have in my possession a slip of paper proving the legality of our relationship.'

'I mean—could we do it again,' Sally explained carefully. 'In church. Not with any guests,' she decried in a rush. 'Just the two of us. If we must have anyone there, Daddy or Carlo—no one else.' There was little she could tell from his expression, and she looked up at him anxiously. 'Would you mind very much?'

Luke's eyes gentled, and he touched her lips with his own. 'If that is what you want, it shall be done just as soon as I can make the necessary arrangements,' he promised quietly.

'Of course,' she began with an impish smile, 'being married already does have its advantages.' She put her head to one side and her eyes sparkled with humour. 'You won't have to sleep elsewhere in the meantime.'

For that observation she was kissed nearly breathless.

'Six lonely nights without you, *cara*,' he husked softly as he swung her up into his arms. '*Dio*, how I have missed you!'

Sally buried her face against his throat, loving the possessive tightening of the arms that held her. 'I don't think I could bear to spend any more time apart from you,' she whispered shakily. 'To wake in the dark and find only an empty space beside me was just —awful.'

'From now on, you will accompany me wherever I go,' Luke vowed firmly, and Sally lifted her head so that she could see his expression.

'Even when I'm pregnant?' she queried teasingly.

'Minx,' he accused fondly as he lowered her down to stand in front of him a few feet from the bed. 'Especially when you are with child.'

'That will cramp your style, won't it?' She pondered thoughtfully, 'A doting papa to two or three little *bambini*, with one very pregnant wife in tow. Ah, whatever will Carmela, Chantrelle, and all the—ouch!' She yelped as his hand made sharp contact with her bottom. 'That hurt!'

'It was meant to,' Luke mocked quizzically. 'You know very well that Carmela, and others like her, ceased to exist for me from the first moment I set eyes on you.'

'I can't think why,' Sally puzzled with complete

lack of guile. 'My face isn't classical—my nose is too small, and my mouth too large. Even my hair can't make up its mind whether to grow straight or to curl. I can cook, though,' she concluded modestly, and her eyes widened as his mouth curved into a gentle smile.

'I will never let you go, *cara*,' he vowed softly. 'Without you, I am only half alive.' His lips sought hers, and it was several minutes before he raised his head.

A sudden irrelevant thought occurred to her, and she asked shakily, 'Have you had dinner? I didn't think to ask. You must be hungry.'

Luke gave a soft laugh as his hands reached for the zip fastener at the back of her dress. 'Only for you, *mia sposa—mia innamorata*.'

The Warrender Saga

The most frequently requested series of Harlequin Romances . . . Mary Burchell's Warrender Saga

Each complete novel is set in the exciting world of music and opera, spanning the years from the meeting of Oscar and Anthea in *A Song Begins* to his knighthood in *Remembered Serenade*. These nine captivating love stories introduce you to a cast of characters as vivid, interesting and delightful as the glittering, exotic locations. From the tranquil English countryside to the capitals of Europe— London, Paris, Amsterdam—the Warrender Saga will sweep you along in an unforgettable journey of drama, excitement and romance.

The Warrender Saga

The most frequently requested Harlequin Romance series

#980 *A Song Begins*

#1100 *The Broken Wing*

#1244 *When Love Is Blind*

#1405 *The Curtain Rises*

#1508 *Child of Music*

#1587 *Music of the Heart*

#1767 *Unbidden Melody*

#1834 *Song Cycle*

#1936 *Remembered Serenade*

Free *Special Bonus Offer*

Purchase all 9 Warrender Saga novels and receive Mary Burchell's We Followed Our Stars as a Free Bonus.

We Followed Our Stars is the story of two sisters who crossed the Atlantic in the golden days of the 1920s, plunging into the glittering world of the opera . . . and later into the horrible brutality of Hitler's war-torn Europe. It's the real story of Ida Cook, a stenographer who became one of the world's most loved writers of romantic fiction—Mary Burchell.

$1.50 *if purchased separately!*

Complete and mail this coupon today!

Harlequin Reader Service

In U.S.A.
MPO Box 707
Niagara Falls, NY 14302

In Canada
Harlequin Reader Service
Stratford, Ontario N5A 6W2

Please send me the following editions of The Warrender Saga. I am enclosing my check or money order for $1.25 per novel ordered, plus 49¢ to cover postage and handling.

- ☐ 980 A Song Begins
- ☐ 1100 The Broken Wing
- ☐ 1244 When Love Is Blind
- ☐ 1405 The Curtain Rises
- ☐ 1508 Child of Music
- ☐ 1587 Music of the Heart
- ☐ 1767 Unbidden Melody
- ☐ 1834 Song Cycle
- ☐ 1936 Remembered Serenade

BONUS OFFER — *We Followed Our Stars*, Mary Burchell's moving autobiography, is yours ABSOLUTELY FREE when you purchase all nine Warrender Saga novels.
☐ Yes, I have purchased all nine of the above. Please send me my copy of *We Followed Our Stars*.

Number of novels checked _____ @ $1.25 each = $ _____

We Followed Our Stars
Mary Burchell's autobiography _____ x $1.50 $ _____

Postage and handling $ _____.49

New York State and New Jersey residents please
add appropriate sales tax $ _____

TOTAL $ _____

NAME _____
(Please Print)
ADDRESS _____

CITY _____

STATE/PROV _____ ZIP/POSTAL CODE _____

Offer Expires December 31, 1979

A.   PRS 289

Put more love
into your life.
Experience the
wonderful world of...

Harlequin Romances

Six brand-new romantic novels
every month, each one a thrilling
adventure into romance...an
exciting glimpse of exotic lands.

Written by world-famous authors,
these novels put at your fingertips
a fascinating journey into the
magic of love, the glamour of
faraway places.

Don't wait any longer. Buy
them now.

What readers say about Harlequin Romances

"Your books are the best I have ever found."
P.B.*. Bellevue. Washington

"I enjoy them more and more
with each passing year."
J.L.. Spurlockville. West Virginia

"No matter how full and happy life might be,
it is an enchantment to sit
and read your novels."
D.K. Willowdale. Ontario

"I firmly believe that Harlequin Romances
are perfect for anyone who wants to read
a good romance."
C.R.. Akron. Ohio

*Names available on request